Mojo FOR MURDER

ISBN: 978-1-68313-035-2
First Edition
Printed and bound in the USA

Cover and interior design by Kelsey Rice

A BERTIE BIGELOW MYSTERY

Mojo FOR MURDER

CAROLYN MARIE WILKINS

P
Pen-L Publishing
Fayetteville, Arkansas
Pen-L.com

Books by Carolyn Wilkins

~ THE BERTIE BIGELOW MYSTERIES ~

Melody for Murder

Mojo for Murder

~ NONFICTION ~

They Raised Me Up,

Damn Near White

Tips for Singers

Chapter One

"Something terrible is going to happen," Mabel Howard said. She slid into the red plastic booth across from Bertie Bigelow and frowned. "You've got to help me."

"Take a deep breath," Bertie replied. In her ten years running the music program at Metro Community College, Bertie had soothed more than her share of nervous people. "Slow down, and tell me the whole story from the beginning."

"I don't have *time* to go back to the beginning, Bertie! Charley's restaurant has been hexed. Sister Destina says the curse will take effect in six hours." Mabel Howard, a bone-thin woman with a nut-brown complexion, tore at her napkin with exquisitely manicured fingers.

Bertie sighed inwardly. Mabel was sharp as a tack, most of the time. But when it came to anything involving psychics, astrology, Tarot cards, or past lives, the woman was a total fanatic.

"Let me get this straight," Bertie said. "You went to see a psychic, and now you think your husband's restaurant has been cursed?"

"Sister Destina is not just any psychic. She's a spiritual genius," Mabel said. "Of course, she's not really a woman. Technically speaking, Sister Destina is a man, but with a lot of yin energy. He was a woman in his last two lifetimes."

1

Out of respect for her friend's feelings, Bertie refrained from rolling her eyes.

"Sounds like a scam to me, girlfriend," she said. Short and soft-spoken, Bertie Bigelow was just shy of forty with a full bosom, a light-beige complexion, and generous hips. "Did this Destina person give you any concrete information about the curse? Anything at all?"

Mabel glared at Bertie through tear-stained eyes. "I'm not stupid, you know. I would never have believed in the curse if my Grandma Hattie hadn't come back from the dead to warn me. Sister Destina saw my grandmother in a vision—clear as I'm seeing you right now. No one can do that unless they have the gift."

It was just after noon, and the TastyCakes Diner was packed. Bertie flagged down a harassed waitress and ordered a tuna sandwich. Too nervous to eat, Mabel ordered coffee.

"Unless a Black Star banishing ritual is performed in the next six hours, Charley and I are as good as dead," Mabel said.

Bertie raised an eyebrow. "Have you talked to your husband about this?"

"I tried, Bertie. I tried." Mabel upended the sugar dispenser and stirred a river of empty calories into her cup. "When I told him the ritual was going to cost two thousand dollars, Charley hit the ceiling. Said he'd see Sister Destina in hell before he gave her a single dime."

Bertie suppressed a grin. Commonly known as the Hot Sauce King, Mabel's husband was a garrulous, blue-black hulk of a man, whose down-home drawl and folksy manners belied a brilliant mind. Charley Howard's Hot Links Emporium was one of the most popular BBQ restaurants on the South Side of Chicago. Bertie was certain he had not clawed his way to the top by gazing dreamily at the stars. Although he swore he'd turned over a new leaf, Charley was rumored to have gotten his start with some help from mob boss Tony Roselli.

"Two thousand dollars is a lot of money," Bertie said. "How do you know Sister Destina didn't make a mistake? Maybe she got her psychic wires crossed up or something."

"No way," Mabel said. "I've been getting chills all day. Something is out of balance in my psychic field, Bertie. I can feel it."

Bertie Bigelow chewed her sandwich thoughtfully. She didn't for one moment believe that Charley Howard's restaurant was in danger. But Mabel was her friend, and for Bertie, friends were everything. She had no children, and her husband Delroy had been killed in a hit-and-run accident eighteen months ago. Without the support of her friends, Bertie knew her own loneliness would have been unbearable.

She pushed her plate aside and leaned forward.

"Remember Francois Dumas?" she said. "The guy who owned the Club Creole on Ninety-Fifth Street?"

"Of course," Mabel said. "Charley and I used to go dancing there."

"Francois ran a great nightclub—fabulous food, live music. Only problem was, he didn't believe in paying taxes. When the IRS threatened to put him in jail, Delroy negotiated his settlement."

"I remember reading about that," Mabel said. "The *Chicago Defender* called your husband the 'African-American Perry Mason.'"

Bertie smiled. "Delroy was always a little embarrassed about that. You know what a modest person he was. The point is, after the trial, Francois gave my husband a small pouch to wear around his neck."

Mabel's eyes widened. "A mojo hand?"

"I guess so. The thing is supposed to keep away evil spirits. You can borrow it if you want."

"Does it work?"

"Delroy carried it in his pocket for months, but on the day of the accident, he left it sitting on the dresser. Forgot it, I guess."

Overcome by sad memories, Bertie fell silent.

"You keep it," Mabel said. She reached across the table and squeezed her friend on the arm. "That mojo hand was made 'specially for Delroy. It wouldn't work for me, anyway."

"You sure?"

Mabel nodded. "Without Sister Destina's Black Star banishing ritual, there's nothing anyone can do."

"Tell you what," Bertie said briskly, "tonight, when I get home from work, I'll dig out the mojo hand and light a candle. Who knows? The thing could still have some whammy left."

"I could certainly use some good vibes," Mabel said with a weak smile. "I know you think I'm crazy, but mark my words, Bertie. Something bad is going to happen tonight."

Chapter Two

Bertie loved teaching at Metro Community College. Located in the heart of Chicago's impoverished South Side, its bunker-like campus was surrounded by vacant lots and boarded-up homes. Occasionally she'd wonder what it would be like to teach full-time students—students who didn't have to work three jobs to put themselves through school. But Metro's campus hummed with the purposeful activity of young people determined to beat the odds. Deep down, Bertie knew it was the place where she was meant to be.

As Bertie poured herself a cup of coffee in the faculty lounge, Ellen Simpson tapped her on the shoulder.

"Can we talk in private, Bertie? I need your advice about something."

Bertie nodded and led the way to her tiny, windowless office at the end of the hall. Ellen had been her best friend since the two of them began teaching at Metro ten years ago. On the surface, Bertie thought, she and Ellen had very little in common. Bertie straightened her hair and wore suits to work. Ellen, on the other hand, sported a no-nonsense Afro and clothing that made her stand out among her colleagues in the English department like a tropical toucan in a pigeon coop.

5

"The College Events Committee has denied my proposal again," Ellen said. She heaved a dramatic sigh and propped herself on the corner of Bertie's desk. "Maybe I should just shoot myself."

Bertie clucked sympathetically. "I know you had your heart set on hosting that conference on hip-hop poetry, but you must have known George Frayley wasn't going to go for it."

"The man is a dinosaur," Ellen said. "He was Illinois Poet Laureate in 1990. But when it comes to the contemporary scene, Frayley hasn't got a clue. Why they made him Events Committee chairman, I'll never know."

"Have you thought about negotiating a compromise?" Bertie said. "Make Frayley the featured poet at your conference. Bet he'd be happy to approve your event then."

"Have you lost your natural mind?" Ellen's voice rose an octave. "The students would hate it. The man's poetry is completely abstract. Even I don't understand it."

"Perhaps," Bertie said mildly. "But at least you'd get the event funded."

Ellen burst out laughing. "Beneath that placid exterior lurks an evil genius worthy of Machiavelli," she said. "Speaking of devious acts, where did you scurry off to after class this morning?"

"Had a very interesting lunch with Mabel Howard."

As Bertie described the encounter, she braced herself in anticipation of a sarcastic response. Ellen was famous for her incisive mind and relentless logic. It seemed unlikely she'd have anything good to say about hoodoo, hexes, or the Black Star banishing ritual.

But Ellen surprised Bertie by nodding thoughtfully.

"It's probably a scam, Bertie, but you never know. The universe is full of mysteries." She lifted herself off the edge of Bertie's desk and readjusted her African head wrap. "Light a candle for your friend. Just in case."

"Maybe I should wave that mojo hand over my choir while I'm at it," Bertie said. "In less than a week, The Ace of Spades will be here to rehearse with us."

"An event I do not intend to miss," Ellen said. "The Ace is one fine-looking man. He hasn't had a hit song in ten years. But when he sings those high notes? My, my, *my!*"

Bertie grinned. "You sure it's the singing you're interested in?"

"Can't say I mind the part where he takes his shirt off and throws it into the audience," Ellen said. "Man's got the best six-pack on the South Side. *That's* the kind of event we need at Metro. How on earth did you get the Events Committee to approve it?"

"I didn't," Bertie said. "Chancellor Grant asked me to do a jazz history concert featuring the music of the singers who grew up in our neighborhood. Chaka Khan, Dinah Washington, Nat King Cole, that sort of thing. Since most folks under thirty have no idea who those people are, Chancellor Grant asked The Ace to lend his star power to the show."

"I'd forgotten he went to school here," Ellen said.

Bertie nodded. "Class of 2000. Graduated just before I got here. He's doing our concert as a special favor to the chancellor. If my kids are not at the top of their game next week, I am toast."

In the middle of choir practice later that afternoon, Bertie threw her music to the floor in disgust.

"Sopranos! We've been over this passage at least ten times. If this is the best you can do, I'm going to tell The Ace to stay home. Are you listening to me?" Bertie shot a penetrating glance at a lanky kid sporting a do-rag in the back row. "Maurice Green. Is that chewing gum I see in your mouth?"

"No, ma'am," Green said. "I was just swallowing."

The boy next to him snickered until Bertie speared him with a glare.

"This is no joke, people," she said. "If we mess this concert up, it will be the last time Chancellor Grant *ever* takes a chance on us. Is that really what you want, Maurice?"

"No, ma'am," the boy muttered. With an awkward shrug, he walked to the front of the room, spat a wad of gum into the wastebasket, and returned to his position in the tenor section.

"All right then," Bertie said. She took a deep breath, retrieved her sheet music from the floor, and nodded to the pianist. "One more time, from the second verse."

Bertie was exhausted when she got home from work that night. She threw off her coat, stuck a Lean Cuisine chicken dinner into the microwave, poured herself a glass of red wine, and pointed her remote at the TV. Like a zombie, she cycled through the channels while she waited for her dinner to heat up. Although her cable package contained at least five hundred channels, Bertie could not find anything even remotely worth watching. Tired reruns of '60s sitcoms competed with reality TV shows highlighting every form of human frailty. If these offerings didn't tickle Bertie's fancy, she had her choice of televangelists preaching in Spanish, English, and Portuguese. Or if she were really looking for a miracle, she could check out the Fast Track Weight Loss infomercial. After all, who didn't want to lose fifty pounds in three weeks?

Bertie was just about to turn off the television when the red brick façade of Charley Howard's Hot Links Emporium flashed across the screen. Channel Four News reporter Lana Ventura stood in front of the building wearing a crisp, navy power suit and a concerned expression.

"A health scare has diners at a popular South Side restaurant fearing for their lives," Ventura announced solemnly. As she spoke, the camera zoomed in on the dancing pigs stenciled on the Emporium's door, giving them a faintly sinister aspect. "Leroy Jefferson, chairman of the Chicago Zoning Board, collapsed during dinner at Howard's Hot Links Emporium earlier this evening. Doctors at Mercy

Hospital have confirmed that the commissioner is being treated for a rare form of bacterial food poisoning. *Staphylococcus aureus* is an unusually fast-acting toxin that can take effect in as little as thirty minutes. At a press conference earlier this evening, the owner of the Hot Links Emporium issued the following statement."

Bertie stared in stunned disbelief as the scene shifted to reveal Charley Howard, standing behind the bar in his restaurant. Sweating profusely, Howard was dressed in his trademark down-home overalls, checked flannel shirt, and white chef's hat. Although Mabel's husband was six inches taller and fifty pounds heavier than most of reporters in the room, he appeared uncharacteristically vulnerable— a bear that had inadvertently stepped on a hornet's nest.

"*All* our food is prepared to the highest standard," Howard insisted. "You can ask anybody. That's why they call me the Hot Sauce King."

As the reporters continued to pepper him with questions, Howard lifted his hands in supplication.

"Please, fellas," he hollered into the din. "I haven't got a single notion how bacteria got into the commissioner's Soul Food Special. I'm as poleaxed by this situation as the rest of you guys."

But the Hot Sauce King's placating expression soured abruptly when a reporter from the *Chicago Sun-Times* asked if Howard had discussed the situation with mob boss Tony Roselli.

"Roselli's got nothin' to do with this," the Hot Sauce King replied.

"That's not what I heard," the reporter insisted. He stepped forward and stuck his microphone under Howard's nose. "Word is, you and Roselli are old friends. Care to comment?"

"I oughta break your neck," Howard growled. His massive fists clenched and unclenched as he struggled to maintain his temper. "Folks, this here powwow is concluded. Immediately. Y'all got two minutes to clear the hell off my property before I phone the law."

Abruptly, the scene shifted to the exterior of the restaurant.

"There you have it, ladies and gentlemen," Lana Ventura said with a sad shake of her head. "Charley Howard threatening reporters while Commissioner Jefferson hovers between life and death. In a related story, the Board of Health has ordered Howard's Hot Links Emporium shut down pending an official investigation. Back to you, Jack."

Bertie Bigelow snapped off her TV, grabbed her cell phone, and punched in Mabel Howard's number. When Mabel did not answer, Bertie fired off a text message.

Just heard the news. Call me anytime.

It was after midnight by the time Bertie crawled into bed. She was nearly asleep when she realized she'd forgotten to light Mabel's candle. Should she get up and dig out the mojo hand? As she wrestled with her conscience, Bertie snuggled deeper under the covers. There was no way that lighting a candle could have prevented this evening's unfortunate incident. She'd only made the offer in a desperate attempt to soothe Mabel's fears. *No,* Bertie told herself as she drifted off to sleep, *this whole sad business was simply a bizarre coincidence.*

Chapter Three

SATURDAY, OCTOBER 14—8:00 AM

The telephone rang as Bertie sat down to breakfast the next morning.

"Got a minute?" Charley Howard's Southern drawl was unmistakable.

"Of course," Bertie said. "I heard about what happened at the restaurant. You guys okay?"

"It's been hell," the Hot Sauce King said bleakly. "I need you to help me fix this thing."

"Fix it? I'm not a health inspector, and Lord knows I'm no public relations specialist."

"I've got a passel full of suits to do my PR," Charley said impatiently. "I need you to do something special. Something no one else can do."

"Okay, Charley, I'll bite. What is it?"

The Hot Sauce King lowered his customarily booming baritone to a whisper. "You know my wife's been seeing this psychic, right?"

"Mabel told me all about Sister Destina," Bertie said. "She thinks the woman has tremendous psychic power."

Charley snorted in disgust. "Psychic power, my foot! The broad's out to get me. It's the only possible explanation for what happened last night. Destina must have paid someone to poison the commissioner's food."

"That would certainly explain the accuracy of her prediction."

"Damn right it would," Charley said. "When the Emporium opened, I put a pair of plastic pigs up on the roof. Within a week, Commissioner Jefferson's people made me take them down. Against zoning regulation H241, they said. The guy's a total fussbudget with a major burr up his butt. What are the odds that, out of all the customers in my restaurant, he's the only person who gets sick?"

"When you put it like that, it does seem suspicious."

"You got that right," Charley said. "Sister Destina is a fake. Problem is, she's got some kind of hold over my wife. Mabel doesn't blow her nose until she's talked to her. Any two-bit detective could expose the woman. But unless the debunking is done by someone she trusts, my wife will never believe it."

"You want me convince Mabel that Sister Destina is a fraud?"

"Darn tootin'," Howard chortled.

In her mind's eye, Bertie pictured the Hot Sauce King's massive ebony face grinning from ear to ear.

"You are a natural busybody, Bertie Bigelow. After Judge Green was murdered last year, you butted your nose into my business big time."

"You know that was never my intention, Charley. I just—"

"No need to protest, little lady. You poked around until the real criminal was found. Compared to catching a cold-blooded murderer, getting the goods on this jive-ass transvestite will be child's play. To sweeten the deal, I'll pay you whatever fee you ask."

"What if Mabel finds out you've got me looking into this thing? She might not like it, you know."

"I'm up against the wall here, dammit!" After a short pause, the Hot Sauce King continued in a plaintive voice. "Last year, Mabel and I found out we couldn't have children. We've been talking about adopting a little girl. Since Destina showed up, Mabel hasn't mentioned adoption once. My wife is turning into a stranger, Bertie. Don't know if she even loves me anymore."

"Of course she does," Bertie said firmly. "Give me Destina's phone number. I think I would like to meet this woman."

For the rest of the weekend, the local media feasted on what it now referred to as the "Hot Links Health Scare." Like a recurring nightmare, clips of Charley Howard telling reporters to "clear the hell off" his property played over and over on local TV. The good news was that Commissioner Jefferson was no longer in critical condition. The bad news was that Jefferson, a small man with a fastidious manner and the physique of a chocolate Easter egg, was furious.

From his hospital bed, the commissioner announced the formation of a special task force to investigate the matter.

"I've eaten in some of the dirtiest cities in the world," he told reporters. "Bangkok. Manila. Phnom Penh. But I never got sick. Not once. Not until I dined in Mr. Howard's benighted establishment."

When asked why he'd chosen to visit the Hot Links Emporium that night, Jefferson said, "One of my student interns suggested it. Said we'd be sure to have a memorable experience."

As the camera pulled in for a close-up, the commissioner pulled himself erect. "Shame, shame, *shame*, Mr. Howard," he said with an admonitory shake of his finger. "You are in violation of Regulation H-255Z. You will be punished to the full extent of the law."

Late Sunday night, Bertie called Sister Destina's number and asked to make an appointment. The voice that answered the phone was soft and high-pitched with a slight lisp. It could have belonged to either a man or a woman.

"Come Tuesday night at six," the voice said. "It's first come, first serve. But as long as you're in the waiting room by six, Sister Destina will see you, no matter how late it gets."

13

Chapter Four

MONDAY, OCTOBER 16—9:00 AM

When Bertie Bigelow walked into the faculty lounge the following morning, she saw Maria Francione standing by the coffee machine. Francione was a buxom redhead who favored low-cut madras tops, tight pants, and stiletto heels. With her loud voice and penchant for sweeping hand gestures, she'd always impressed Bertie as a drama teacher right out of Central Casting.

"Have you looked at the paper today?" Francione asked.

Bertie shook her head. The last thing she wanted to see that morning were the headlines. All weekend, the *Chicago Sun-Times* had run stories about the Hot Links Health Scare. Yesterday's offering had been a gossipy feature titled "Celebrities and Salmonella," listing various Chicago luminaries who had contracted food poisoning recently. At the top of the list was Zoning Board Commissioner Leroy Jefferson, who was described as "recovering nicely" from the incident.

Ignoring Bertie's unenthusiastic expression, Francione reached into her oversized shoulder bag, extracted a copy of the *Chicago Sun-Times*, and thrust it into Bertie's hand.

"Don't bother with the front page," she said. "It's all bad news anyway. Turn to the Arts and Culture section, page 8-D."

While Francione peered anxiously over her shoulder, Bertie opened the paper and began to read.

LOCAL TEACHER STARS IN ONE-WOMAN SHOW
Tomorrow at 8:00 pm, the Goodman Theater Workshop will present a reading of **Basta, Mama!** Maria Francione, an associate professor of theater arts at Metro Community College, wrote, directed, and produced the play. She will also be performing the title role.

"Congratulations," Bertie said. She put down the paper and gave her colleague a hug. "If I didn't already have an appointment tomorrow evening, I would definitely be there."

"An appointment? What could possibly be more important than the one-and-only performance of my new show?"

Although Francione laughed, Bertie could tell that, at some level, the woman was serious. Having spent the majority of her life around performers, Bertie recognized the sound of a bruised ego when she heard it.

"Sorry, Maria. Really. I am sure you will be fantastic, but I'm going to see a psychic tomorrow night."

"A psychic?" Francione covered her eyes. Adopting a ridiculously fake Hungarian accent she intoned, "I see a tall, dark, and handsome man in your future, Mrs. Bigelow. Someone with deep, soulful eyes and rippling muscles. Most important of all, I see a beautiful Italian actress receiving rave reviews for her performance at the Goodman Theater."

Bertie grinned. "I don't know about the tall, dark, and handsome part, but I'm sure your play is going to be a smash. I'm really sorry I won't be able to make it."

Francione waved her hand grandly. "Some other time, my dear. Perhaps when I'm on Broadway. In the meanwhile, do me a favor and give these comp tickets to your students. I'm at my best when I perform for a full house."

With a grin, Bertie took the tickets, poured herself of cup of coffee, and carried it back down the hallway. With any luck, she'd be able to answer a few emails and organize her lecture notes before her next class.

As Bertie approached her office, she saw a tall, willowy girl with shoulder-length hair leaning against the wall. The girl wore a pair of designer skinny jeans, a loose-fitting white blouse, sunglasses, and a Bulls cap propped at a jaunty angle. Bertie sighed and mentally said goodbye to her plans of getting organized before class. Nyala Clark, Metro's reigning student diva, was waiting for her.

"I simply cannot sing under these conditions," Nyala announced and swept into Bertie's office.

"What could possibly be the matter so early in the morning," Bertie said.

"I'm talking about my solo, of course." Nyala plopped her over-sized handbag unceremoniously in the center of Bertie's desk. "The whole thing is beyond stupid."

"What whole thing, Nyala?" Bertie didn't like to start her day with drama and conflict, but as the director of a fifty-voice choir, she had grown used to dealing with high-strung performers. "Why don't you start from the beginning. Tell me exactly what's on your mind."

The problem was that Nyala's solo at the end of their upcoming concert had been cut to make room for a hip-hop dance number featuring Nyala's archrival, Melissa Jones.

"Jamz Management is considering me for a part in their next Mega Funk tour," Nyala said. "That song was supposed to be my showcase."

Bertie felt a vein begin to throb in her right temple. "I understand how you feel, Nyala, but the concert is not just about you. It's a show-case for the entire choral program. The Ace has specifically asked that a dance number be included in our show."

"Did you ever stop to think why?" Nyala shot back, her eyes flashing. "Why The Ace wants dancing all of a sudden?"

"I'm sure he has his reasons."

"Oh, he's got *reasons,* all right." Nyala's voice dripped with sarcasm. "The Ace wants dancing 'cause that skank Melissa Jones *sexted* him, Mrs. B! Sent the man a photo of herself bare-ass naked."

Bertie sighed. For the most part, she loved her students and loved her job, but there were times when she wished she'd heeded her father's advice and gotten an MBA instead. This morning was definitely shaping up to be one of them.

"And you know this how?"

"Everybody knows it. Everybody but you, of course. Ask Melissa yourself if you don't believe me."

"I will do that," Bertie said crisply. She pushed back her chair and stood up. "Regardless of what I find out, the best way to help yourself is to sing like an absolute goddess. The Ace sees plenty of naked girls in his line of work. But a great singer? That, my dear, is one in a million."

The rest of Bertie's day unfolded with similar intensity. Her Theory 101 students did poorly on the quiz she'd given the week before. Two boys from her History of Western Music seminar sent her emails to complain about their grades.

Worst of all, Melissa Jones was a no-show at choir rehearsal that afternoon.

Could it be that Nyala's allegations were true? By the time Bertie had finished her last class, she was simply too tired to care. She sent Melissa an email, instructing the girl to stop by her office as soon as possible. The next day, first thing, she'd check with the dean of students and see what else needed to be done. But for the moment, Bertie Bigelow's working day was over.

She had gotten in the habit of stopping off at Rudy's Tap on her way home from work. Although it was just a grungy hole in the wall, the bar provided a welcome refuge on those nights when she dreaded returning directly from the bustle of Metro to the silence of an empty home. The lights were kept low to disguise the peeling paint and weathered tables, and, barring an absolute emergency, no one in their right mind ever used the restroom. But the place had the best jukebox on the South Side of Chicago. At Rudy's, the serious music lover could find anything that suited his mood, whether it was a ballad by Billie Holiday, a down-home blues by B.B. King, or a Motown classic from Stevie Wonder.

R. Kelly was crooning something slow and sexy as Bertie slid onto a stool at the bar. After ordering her usual Merlot, she spotted Ellen Simpson sitting alone at a table in the back. Dressed in a lime-green dashiki, matching head wrap, and a glittering pair of ankh-shaped earrings, Simpson was easily visible, in spite of the bar's dim lighting.

"Hey girl," Bertie said, walking over to join her. "You'll never guess what I just found out." When Bertie had finished telling her friend about Melissa Jones and the sexting incident, Ellen shook her head sadly.

"Kids these days are crazy," Ellen said. "And it's not just the kids. Truth is, everybody's crazy. There's no honor, no loyalty, and no morals left. I'm telling you, Bertie. Society is going to hell in a handbasket."

Until that moment, Bertie had been completely immersed in her own troubles, but something about Ellen's bleak tone and pessimistic remarks caught her attention.

"That doesn't sound at all like you, Ellen. What are you doing here, anyway? I thought Jerome was taking you out to dinner tonight."

Only last week, Ellen had said that, if Jerome ever popped "the question," she would answer in the affirmative.

"I am through with that jive-time jerk forever," Ellen said bitterly. "Don't even speak his name."

"What happened?"

"Young-Mi Kim happened," Ellen said. "Jerome and I were getting it on every Saturday night, but he had a whole other flavor happenin' during the week."

"Say what?"

"You heard me. Brother was steppin' out with this little Korean chick behind my back. The man had the absolute nerve to call at three o'clock this morning to tell me all about it." A tear slid down Ellen's cheek and splashed into her rum and Coke. "He says he's going to marry this woman."

"I know how much you were hoping he'd be the one," Bertie said softly.

She took the cocktail napkin from under her wine glass and pressed it into her best friend's hand.

"The worst thing is, I had absolutely no idea," Ellen said, shaking her head. "None whatsoever."

"You know what they say. Hindsight is always twenty-twenty."

"I've had it, Bertie. I am through with men." Ellen raised her glass in mock salute. "To celibacy!"

"Don't be silly," Bertie said. "A month from now, you'll have moved on completely. Last time you broke up with a guy, you met someone new the next day. Remember?"

"It's not going to take me a month to move on this time, girlfriend. I plan to forget that sorry-ass chump immediately." Ellen tipped back her head, polished off the rest of her drink in one long swallow, and stood up. "Lemme get us another round."

"Hold on a minute," Bertie said. "You do remember what happened the last time you got drunk, right?"

Ellen cracked a wry smile and sat down. "I passed out in a plate of chicken wings, as I recall. Maybe you're right. Maybe I don't want to do that again."

"Of course not," Bertie said. "You just need something else to occupy your mind." She pushed aside her drink and leaned forward. "Remember Sister Destina, the fortune teller I told you about?"

"How could I forget?" Ellen said. "Charley Howard's restaurant has been all over the news. Couldn't have picked a worse guy to poison. Commissioner Jefferson is a real stickler for regulations."

"So I've heard."

"Guy's some kind of Asia nut—always talking about his trips to the Exotic East. But traveling doesn't seem to have helped his disposition any. Rumor has it he sleeps with the Chicago Zoning Code under his pillow at night." Ellen took a swallow of her drink before continuing. "Lord knows he's not sleeping with his wife. Alvitra Jefferson's got a face like a hog, a tongue like a razor, and a disposition that would piss off the Dalai Lama. People only put up with her because she's H.L.R. Swade's daughter."

"*The* H.L.R. Swade?"

Ellen nodded. "The very same. Founder of Swade Insurance Group—the oldest and largest African-American insurance company in the Midwest. Daddy Swade spoiled his daughter rotten, and she expects the same treatment from her husband. You know the deal—a new Cadillac every year, and a fur coat to go with it. No wonder Commissioner Jefferson is a tyrant in his pathetic little world. That's what happens when you're not getting any nookie."

Bertie flushed and looked away.

"Present company excepted, of course."

Bertie waved Ellen's apology aside. "Charley's restaurant has been shut down by the Board of Health."

"I pity the guy assigned to put up that 'Closed' sign," Ellen said. "The Hot Sauce King's got one hell of a temper."

"Don't I know it," Bertie said. "You should have heard him Saturday night. He thinks Sister Destina is running some kind of protection racket."

"Why doesn't he have the Roselli brothers pay the woman a visit? One look at those goons and she'll be on the next plane out of town."

"Charley swears he's no longer connected to the Mob," Bertie said. "Says his business is strictly on the up-and-up, and you know what? I believe him. He's been a changed man ever since he got accepted into the Octagon Society."

"The Octagons call themselves *the most exclusive* black social club in Chicago," Ellen said, pulling a sour face. "Bunch of color-struck snobs, if you ask me."

"Perhaps," Bertie said. "But they don't tolerate any funny business. A person's got to mind their Ps and Qs if they want to fit in with that set."

"Wearing that goofy checked shirt and a pair of overalls? Charley's got a ways to go in the social decorum department," Ellen said wryly. "But I do take your point. A close association with the Mob might be a bit over the top for those uppity Octagon Negroes."

"Charley may be a loudmouthed tough guy, but where Mabel's concerned, the man's a total cream puff," Bertie said. "He worships the ground she walks on. I've never seen him this worried. Apparently, Mabel has stopped talking to him. Spends all her time on the phone with Sister Destina."

"Think Mabel's under some kind of spell?"

"Charley's asked me to look into it," Bertie said. "I've got an appointment to see this Destina person tomorrow night. Want to come along?"

Ellen cocked her head to one side. "See a fortune teller? Me?"

"It'll be fun," Bertie said. "Take your mind off your problems."

"Well, I suppose you've got a point about that," Ellen said with a smile. "What have I got to lose? If she's any good, maybe she can hook me up with a love potion or something. God knows I could use it."

Chapter Five

Bertie was grading papers in her office when Melissa Jones walked in the following morning. The girl wore a leather miniskirt that left little to the imagination. Shiny purple lipstick, thigh-high boots, and a skimpy red tank top completed the outfit. Without waiting for an invitation, she settled herself in the chair opposite Bertie's desk.

"You wanted to see me, Mrs. B?"

"There's a rumor going around that you sent nude photos of yourself to The Ace of Spades," Bertie said. "Is it true?"

"Is that what this is about?" Melissa's tinkling laugh reminded Bertie of Glinda, the Good Witch. "I was afraid I'd done something wrong—you know, flunked a test or something."

Bertie took a deep breath while mentally picking her jaw up off the floor. "So you admit it?"

"Sure," Melissa said. "It's not illegal, you know."

"Aren't you concerned you'll be giving The Ace the wrong impression?"

"Just making the most of my assets," Melissa said with a shrug. "Give him something to think about. Maybe he'll have a part for me in his next video."

"Sexting is not appropriate behavior, Melissa. Not at Metro College, and certainly not in my choir," Bertie said. "I'm going to have to report this to the dean of students."

Melissa's expression darkened. "This ain't even your business, Mrs. B. I'm over eighteen, and so is The Ace. It's a free country, you know."

"The country may be free, but my choir is not," Bertie said firmly. "Unless Doctor Witherspoon says otherwise, you are suspended from choir practice until further notice."

With surprising speed for someone so tightly encased in leather clothing, Melissa Jones ran out of Bertie's office and slammed the door behind her.

In the silence that followed, Bertie sighed heavily. After a moment, she gathered up her briefcase and rode Metro's creaking old elevator six floors up to the office of the dean of student affairs.

"Come in, Professor Bigelow, come in," Dr. Terrance Witherspoon said. The new dean was tall and lanky with skin the color of spun caramel. Though his mustache and close-cropped hair were peppered with gray, he carried himself with the ease of a man in his early thirties. "Have a seat. I gather it's urgent or you wouldn't have dropped by like this."

Although he'd only been on the job for a few weeks, Witherspoon projected an air of confidence, listening calmly as Bertie poured out her story. When she had finished, he smiled.

"Believe it or not, we had a similar incident at Minneapolis College last year." The dean's voice was deep, and his delivery was leisurely, as though he had all the time in the world. "Sexting between consenting adults may be in bad taste, but it is not against the law." Witherspoon chuckled softly. "Welcome to the twenty-first century, Professor."

As a wave of relief swept over her, Bertie smiled. Before Witherspoon's arrival, she would have had to discuss the sexting incident directly with Chancellor Grant, a compulsive micromanager who tended to turn even the smallest anthill into Mt. Everest. The new dean's relaxed approach was a welcome breath of fresh air. *What's more,* Bertie thought to herself, *the man is definitely easy on the eyes.*

"So what happens next?" she said. "The Ace of Spades is coming to campus for a rehearsal next week. I'd sure like to have this resolved before he arrives."

"I'll give our little extrovert a phone call," Witherspoon said. "With any luck, I'll be able to work out a solution in the next day or two."

As he ushered Bertie out of his office, she couldn't help but notice that the new dean smelled faintly of musk. Was it her imagination, or did their parting handshake linger a beat longer than the accepted norm?

That evening, as they drove to their appointment with Sister Destina, Bertie told Ellen about her encounter with Dr. Witherspoon.

"Something about the way he shook my hand felt strange," Bertie said.

She flipped on her turn signal and guided her Honda down the ramp and onto the Dan Ryan Expressway. The Dan Ryan cut a wide swath through the city's black neighborhoods, a fact that had not gone unnoticed by African-American conspiracy theorists. To this day, some South Siders whispered that the highway's route had been deliberately altered to keep blacks out of Mayor Richard J. Daley's all-white Bridgeport neighborhood.

"Watch out for that truck," Ellen said, her hands twisting nervously in her lap. "If he changes lanes, he'll wipe us out in a heartbeat." Fearless in most situations, Ellen was an absolute shrinking violet when it came to driving.

"Relax, girlfriend. I've got my eye on it. What I'm asking you is, should I be keeping an eye on Terrance Witherspoon? Sure felt like there was more than a handshake going on this afternoon."

Ellen cocked her head and flashed Bertie a knowing look. "How long has it been, Bert?"

"How long since what?"

"You know."

Bertie blushed. "Not since Delroy died last April."

"Your husband was one in a million," Ellen said. "But he's gone, and you are barely forty. It's time you started thinking about dating again."

Bertie sighed. "I suppose you're right, but I've been out of the meat market for eleven years. I wouldn't even know how to begin."

"All the more reason for you to jump into the pool as soon as possible," Ellen said. As she rubbed her hands together, the copper bracelets she always wore jangled merrily. "That new dean is a fine-looking specimen. I wouldn't mind doing a few laps in the pool with him myself."

"I ought to wash your mouth out with soap," Bertie said, laughing.

"Seriously, Bertie. Pheromones don't lie. Your feminine intuition was right on the money about that handshake. The man is attracted to you. And what's more, you are attracted to him."

Bertie contemplated this new idea in silence for several minutes as she maneuvered her car off the highway and turned onto Ninety-Fifth Street.

"Maybe you're right," she said softly. "It's been so long, I can hardly feel myself down there."

Ellen grinned wickedly. "I bet the good dean has got a remedy for that."

"Your mind stays in the gutter," Bertie said. "Why don't you take a look at that map on your cell phone? Destina's street should be coming up on the left in two blocks."

Chapter Six

The first thing Bertie noticed about Destina's house was the smell. A combination of melting candle wax, human sweat, incense, and cheap cologne filled the psychic's tiny living room-cum-reception area with an indefinable and somewhat exotic funk. Although it was a relatively warm October day, the psychic's furnace was running full blast. On the wall opposite the front door, red velvet curtains bordered with gold tassels covered the room's only window. On the adjacent wall, a dozen candles in glass containers flickered underneath a large velvet portrait of Jesus on the cross. The only other light in the room was provided by a faux-Tiffany lamp perched on the table at one end of the ornate French provincial sofa that sat underneath the window.

As her eyes adjusted to the gloom, Bertie noticed a white woman in a pink L'Etiole tennis dress sitting on the sofa. The woman was slim and looked to be in her mid-forties. Her short blonde hair had been carefully layered, and she radiated the athletic glow of someone not accustomed to missing her daily workout.

"Don't just stand there, you two," the woman said. "Sit down."

"We're here to see Sister Destina," Bertie said hastily and extended her hand. "I'm Bertie Bigelow, and this is my friend Ellen Simpson."

As she walked toward the couch, Bertie heard Ellen mutter something under her breath. Ellen was notoriously quick to take offense when she felt she was being bossed around—especially if the bossy person happened to be white.

"Penny Swift." The white woman leaned forward slightly to offer a brisk handshake. "This your first time?"

Bertie nodded.

"I wouldn't miss my session with Destina for all the tea in China," Penny said. "My driver brings me up here twice a week from Kenilworth."

"It's a fifty mile round trip from Kenilworth to Morgon Park," Ellen said sharply. "Don't they have psychics out in the suburbs?"

Penny laughed. "Not like Destina. That woman can work miracles."

As Ellen grunted and took a seat on the couch, Bertie studied Penny Swift thoughtfully. Her crisp accent, pampered body, and designer clothes reeked of privilege. Nevertheless, the woman exuded an unmistakable air of sadness. Her carefully applied makeup could not completely hide the lines under her eyes. And despite an expensive manicure, the nails on her fingers had been chewed to the quick.

"Mabel Howard tells me the same thing," Bertie said. "She swears by Destina's predictions."

"Mabel's a friend of yours?"

Bertie nodded.

"Mabel Howard is my *homie*," the white woman said, affecting a Southern accent without a trace of irony. "Haven't seen her since the incident, though. How's she holding up?"

"'Bout as well as you would expect," Bertie replied, "considering."

Penny shook her head sadly. "The whole tragedy could have been averted, you know. If Destina had been allowed to do her banishing ritual, Howard's Hot Links Emporium would be open for business right now."

Ellen Simpson had been squirming in her seat for the past several minutes. She was here to support Bertie, and the last thing she wanted was to get in a shouting match with the white woman at the other end of the sofa. But Penny's last statement was just too damn much.

"Don't be silly," Ellen snapped. "It was a simple case of food poisoning. Could have happened to anybody."

Penny favored Ellen with a smug smile. "But it didn't happen to *just* anybody, did it? It happened in Charley Howard's restaurant. Just the way Sister Destina predicted it."

Ellen shook her head and grunted like a bull preparing to charge.

"That's all very interesting," Bertie said, shooting a warning glance in Ellen's direction. "But I'm curious. How did you find out about Sister Destina?"

"My driver, Cedric, recommended her. I used to have a terrible problem going to sleep at night. My husband took me to a sleep specialist, who put me on every drug in the book. Ambien, Lunesta, Rozerem—you name it. I've had psychotherapy. I've had hypnotherapy. I even tried acupuncture, but nothing worked."

"That must have been difficult," Bertie said. "I take it you're feeling much better now?"

"Sister Destina healed me," Penny said. Her blue eyes sparkled with missionary zeal. "I'm telling you, it was a miracle. She identified my problem immediately."

"Fascinating," Bertie said. "Do you mind telling me what the problem was?"

Penny glanced around the room nervously and moved closer before announcing softly, "There was a dark entity stuck to my aura."

As Ellen suppressed a giggle, Bertie nodded blandly. "My, my," she said. "That sounds serious. How did Sister Destina get rid of the entity?"

"That, my dear, is a secret," Penny said. "My tongue will turn black and swell up like a goiter if I tell a single soul. Anyway, I'm not completely healed just yet. Sister Destina says I still need more work."

"Sounds like a complicated case," Bertie said. "Do you know if Mabel had entities as well?"

Penny shook her head. "We're not encouraged to share the details of our sessions. Kind of like going to the doctor, you know. Patient confidentiality and all that."

At that moment, a door to Bertie's left opened to reveal a heavy-set black man in a rumpled business suit and a young man sporting baggy jeans and a silk do-rag.

"A pleasure, as always, Jabarion," the man said. He clasped the younger man's hand and shook it vigorously. "She's a wonder-work-er, that Destina. An absolute miracle woman."

The younger man, who looked to be somewhere around twenty, arched an eyebrow and offered a frosty smile.

"I'll stop by your office later in the week, Mr. Sweetwater," he lisped in a girlish falsetto. "Meanwhile, have a great evening."

"That I will, son. Now that I've seen Sister Destina, I believe it's going to be a very fine evening indeed." With a hearty laugh, the man threw a black raincoat over his shoulder and strode across the waiting room.

"Have a great session, Penny," he said. With a final wave, the man walked out of the house and slammed the front door behind him.

In the silence that followed, the young man extracted a small bot-tle of hand sanitizer from his pocket, applied a dab to his left palm, and rubbed his hands together. After carefully inspecting each finger, he turned toward the sofa.

"Ready, Mrs. Swift?" he said.

"Of course, Jabarion, darling. How is the diva today? In good spirits?"

"Comme ci, comme ça." The young man wiggled his left hand from side to side. "She's not in one of her moods, if that's what you're worried about. Not yet, anyway."

Like a French courtier from a bad Hollywood melodrama, he glid-ed across the room, took Penny's hand, and kissed it.

"Come with me to the Kasbah, ma chérie," he purred. "Destina's inner sanctum awaits."

"Jabarion Coutze Junior," Penny squealed, her tanned face red with excitement. "Shame on you, flirting with an old lady like that."

Taking Jabarion's arm, Penny waved gaily at Bertie and Ellen and sashayed out of the room.

As the door to Destina's inner sanctum closed behind the unlikely couple, Ellen poked Bertie in the ribs. "We've had some crazy adventures together, but girl, this sho'nuff takes the cake," she said. "Do you have any idea who you're dealing with here?"

"A rich white woman, an effeminate teenager, and a loudmouth fat man," Bertie said. "And that's just for starters."

"You really don't know who these people are?"

"Of course not. Do you?"

"I know you need to practice the piano every day, Bertie, but you're hopelessly uninformed about the really important facts of life. You should read the gossip columns more often."

Bertie shook her head irritably. "If you know something about these folks, you need to tell me. It could be important."

"Okay, okay." Ellen moved closer to Bertie on the couch and lowered her voice to a whisper. "The crazy white woman? Penny Swift? Her family owns the Marshall Swift Department Store chain."

Bertie whistled softly. "She must be paying Sister Destina a fortune for those sessions she's getting."

"No doubt. But she's not the only big fish here," Ellen continued. "The fat guy that just left is Max Sweetwater."

"The real estate tycoon?"

"As I live and breathe. Sleazy SOB was on the news just the other night, announcing a new development at Fifty-Ninth and Wabash. Rumor is, he bought the land for a song last year after a series of suspicious fires in the neighborhood."

"He doesn't seem like the kind of person who'd go to a psychic," Bertie said. "Wonder what he's doing here."

"I have no idea," Ellen said. "But let me tell you something even stranger. The light-skinned boy? That's Jabarion Coutze Junior."

"I *know* that, Ellen. I was sitting right here while Penny was talking to him, remember?"

Ellen gave Bertie a pitying look. "Do I have to fill in all the blanks here? Just think about it for a second. Jabarion Coutze. Where have you heard that name before?"

After a moment, Bertie's eyes widened. "He's related to *the* Jabarion Coutze? The drug lord?"

"That would be my guess. Coutze is not exactly your run-of-the-mill surname."

"Wasn't that the guy they busted on a murder charge last year?"

"That's the one," Ellen said. "Imagine the irony, Bertie. While Daddy is doing consecutive life sentences in the slammer, Junior is hanging around with a cross-dressing psychic and hugging up on white ladies."

As Ellen leaned over to make a further comment, the door leading to Destina's inner sanctum flew open. Penny Swift, her face wet with tears, stormed into the room, grabbed her jacket, and rushed out the front door.

"Sister Destina will see you now," Jabarion announced. His expression was unreadable as he crossed the living room and pulled the front door shut. "Which one of you ladies will be going first?"

"My friend and I have never done this before," Bertie said. "Is it possible for us to go in together?"

"As you wish." Jabarion Coutze lifted his shoulders in a world-weary shrug. "Follow me."

Chapter Seven

Bertie and Ellen looked around in amazement. The light in the psychic's inner sanctum was dazzling. The walls and ceiling of the room had been painted a glossy white, and thick white curtains covered the room's only window. Next to the window was an elaborate triangular bookshelf. On the bottom shelf, flickering white candles alternated with large mason jars filled with an unidentifiable white liquid. The next several shelves contained dark-skinned dolls of both sexes dressed in white clothing, china serving bowls piled high with shredded coconut flakes, and bottles of Bacardi rum that had been painted white to match the décor. At the top of the bookshelf, a large human skull stood upright, surveying the room with hollow eyes.

Jabarion pointed toward two white velvet armchairs sitting in the center of the room. Without further explanation, he turned on his heel and walked out, closing the door behind him. Directly in front of the two chairs was a raised platform flanked by a pair of potted palm trees. In the center of the platform, illuminated by a set of halogen bulbs recessed into the ceiling, sat an elaborate faux-gold throne worthy of Louis XVI.

"Reminds me of the time I played an angel in the Easter pageant," Ellen said with a nervous laugh.

"Except for the skull," Bertie said. "I'm guessing your church did not have one of those."

At that moment, a panel in the wall behind the platform slid open, and an enormous, dark-skinned figure glided into the room.

"I am Sister Destina," the figure announced in a Jamaican-accented baritone. "Welcome."

The psychic wore a white sleeveless wedding gown, long kid gloves, and a shoulder-length blonde wig. Moving with the inexorable grace of a circus elephant, she ascended the two steps that led to the stage and settled herself on the throne.

"I see that you have chosen to be read together," she said.

Feeling a bit like kids being called into the principal's office, Bertie and Ellen nodded sheepishly.

Sister Destina closed her eyes and took a deep breath. For a moment, the room was absolutely silent. Suddenly, she screamed and began to shake. Pushing herself to a standing position, the psychic pointed an accusatory finger in Ellen's direction.

"There is a dark entity attached to your aura," she thundered. As Destina spoke, her massive jowls quivered like Jell-O. "If this condition is not treated immediately, your life is in serious danger."

Ellen's eyes narrowed. "You're telling me I've been cursed?"

"Someone has placed a bondage hex on you," Sister Destina said. "An exorcism must be performed tomorrow. Bring a fresh beef heart, a pinch of graveyard dust, and nine straight pins when you return."

"Hold on just a minute, there. I'm not doing anything till you tell me what's up with this curse." Ellen's copper bracelets jangled as she made air quotes around the word *curse*. "How do I even know it exists? You got any proof?"

"I do not engage in idle banter with skeptics," Destina snapped. She pulled a bloodstained sword from a stand positioned next to her throne. Waving the two-foot steel blade with one hand, she tossed a black Raggedy Anne doll into the air above her head with the other. As Bertie and Ellen watched in amazement, Destina swung the blade, beheading the hapless doll in midair.

"Begone, evil spirit," Destina thundered. "*Exorcizamus te, omnis immundus spiritus.* Leave us!"

"With pleasure," Ellen said. "Let's get the hell out of here, Bertie."

The two women were halfway across the room when the psychic said in a softer voice, "Stay with me a minute, Mrs. Bigelow. I have something important to tell you."

As Bertie hesitated, Ellen turned to face her.

"Want me to stay with you, Bert?"

"No," Bertie said. "I'll be fine. You go ahead."

"Just call out if old fatso here tries to start any funny stuff," Ellen said in a stage whisper. "I'll be right outside."

Once Ellen had left the room, Sister Destina returned the sword to its stand, lumbered off the dais, and lowered her massive bulk into the armchair chair next to Bertie. Although her immense weight, stage makeup, and outlandish costume made it difficult to tell, the psychic appeared to be in her early thirties.

"You think I'm a fake, don't you," she said.

"Let's just say I'm a bit of a skeptic," Bertie replied. "Either way, I can see you're working hard keeping the people entertained."

"You have no idea," Sister Destina said softly. The powder on the psychic's dark, moon-shaped face was streaked with sweat, and circles lined her eyes. "But you didn't come out here to listen to my problems. You came to learn about your own."

Sister Destina folded her hands in her lap and closed her eyes. For at least a minute, the psychic neither moved nor spoke, reminding Bertie of a massive obsidian Buddha she'd once seen at the Art Institute. Except that this Buddha was wearing false eyelashes, a blonde wig, and a wedding dress.

"You have come through the valley of darkness, Bertie." Sister Destina's eyes remained closed, and she spoke gently, as if talking to a child. "The man you loved was taken from you swiftly and without warning nearly two years ago."

Bertie inhaled sharply but remained silent. *Calm yourself, girl-friend. She probably looked you up on Google or something.*

"Delroy wants you to know he's proud of the way you've handled yourself," Destina continued. "But he says it's time for you to move on with your life. He wants you to know it's all right to see other men."

"How can you possibly know this?" Bertie said in a small, frightened voice.

Ignoring Bertie's question, the psychic began to sway rhythmically back and forth.

"You will be approached by three men before the year is out," she chanted in a singsong voice. "An old friend, a new friend, and a false friend. All three men will fall in love with you, but only one will bring you happiness." The psychic's eyes popped open. "You have a powerful talisman, Bertie. You must wear it at all times. I see danger around you."

"Danger? How can you say these things?" Bertie said. "And who are these three men you're talking about? I haven't dated anyone in years."

But Sister Destina merely shook her head.

"Leave me now, Bertie. I'm tired."

Without another word, the psychic levered her massive bulk into a standing position and glided out of the room.

Chapter Eight

After leaving Sister Destina's house, Bertie found herself hungrier than she had ever been in her life. Ellen did not need much convincing when Bertie suggested they stop at Pizza Capri, an upscale Italian restaurant in Hyde Park, for a late dinner.

"After the ridiculous gong show we just witnessed, I am going to need a drink," Ellen said, waving imperiously in the direction of their waiter. "Do you know how much money that jive-ass psychic was going to charge to un-hex me?"

Bertie shook her head and sipped her water absently.

"Five hundred dollars. That's right—five hundred American dollars." Ellen snorted in disgust. "I told that little thug Jabarion Coutze I'd see him in hell first." When the waiter reappeared with Ellen's drink, she grabbed it off his tray and took a long swallow. "Girl, I have never heard so much pure-D horse manure in my entire life."

When Bertie continued to stare into space without replying, Ellen waved a hand in her face.

"Earth to Bertie! Earth to Bertie! What the hell is the matter with you? You've hardly said a word since we got here. Did that phony psychic upset you?"

"I guess you could say that," Bertie said. She looked down and poked at a stray glob of pizza cheese on her plate.

"Out with it, girlfriend." Ellen's copper bracelets clanked impatiently as she leaned forward in her seat. "She tell you you'd been cursed?"

"Not exactly. In a way, it was even scarier. She knew all about Delroy, Ellen. That he had died young—everything. She mentioned him by name."

"Umph," Ellen grunted. "Probably just looked you up on the internet."

Bertie continued to look down at her plate. "She said I need to start dating again."

"Well, duh," Ellen said. "You don't have to be psychic to figure that out. I've been telling you that for months."

"This was different," Bertie said. "She told me that three men would fall in love with me before the end of the year—an old friend, a new friend, and a false friend."

Ellen shook her head impatiently. "It's been damn near two years since you even looked at a man. No offense, but it seems unlikely that you'd suddenly turn into a femme fatale before December. It's already the middle of October, for Pete's sake."

"I suppose you're right," Bertie said.

But for the rest of the evening, she continued to brood about Destina's prediction. Had it been a true message from the beyond? A lucky guess? Or was it merely a carefully planned hoax?

As she lay in bed that night, Bertie dreamed she was being carried out of a burning building by a young Denzel Washington. Depositing her gently on the ground, he leaned over and took her face in his hands. Denzel's breath smelled faintly of mint. His soulful eyes spoke a message that needed no words. As their lips touched, Bertie felt her body melt in a moment of exquisite surrender and—

Beep-beep. Beep-beep. Beep-BEEP! The sound of her alarm clock intruded rudely into Bertie's dream. She hit the snooze button immediately, but it was too late. Denzel had vanished into the ethereal haze from which he'd come, leaving Bertie feeling lonelier than ever.

She dragged herself out of bed, splashed cold water on her face, and rubbed the sleep from her eyes. *Enough of this foolishness. Denzel's not coming to rescue you. Not in this lifetime, girlfriend. Stop daydreaming and get your sorry butt to work.*

Chapter Nine

WEDNESDAY, OCTOBER 18—9:00 AM

The phone on Bertie's desk was ringing when she walked into her office.

"All hell's broken loose," Hedda Eberhardt said. "Stop whatever you're doing and get up here right away."

Bertie's mind churned with anxiety as Metro's slow-as-molasses elevator wheezed its way up to the sixth floor. An unexpected summons from the chancellor's personal secretary at this hour of the morning could not possibly be a good thing. What could be so important that it had to be taken care of immediately? Ten minutes later and only slightly out of breath, Bertie stood in front of Eberhardt's antique desk.

"Melissa Jones' mother stormed in here at eight o'clock this morning and has refused to leave," Eberhardt said. The flat twang of her Chicago accent lent an additional edge to her voice. "The chancellor had no choice but to call an emergency meeting. Go on in. Everyone's waiting for you."

Bertie Bigelow took a deep breath, squared her shoulders, and walked into the executive conference room. Through the floor-to-ceiling glass windows that lined the far wall, she could see that it was shaping up to be a fine October day. She only hoped she would still be among the gainfully employed when the sun went down.

39

Chancellor Humbert Xavier Grant, dressed in a gray Brooks Brothers suit, sat at the head of the oval shaped conference table that dominated the room. A blue silk handkerchief protruded from his breast pocket, and his few remaining strands of suspiciously black hair were pomaded firmly to the top of his dome-shaped head.

"At last," he exclaimed in a majestic baritone. "So glad you could join us, Professor Bigelow."

This does not sound good, Bertie thought to herself. *Not at all.* Was her boss implying that she had deliberately come late to the meeting?

As Bertie stood awkwardly by the door, Terrance Witherspoon, Metro's dean of students, caught her eye and smiled.

"If you ask me, the professor looks a bit out of breath," Witherspoon said easily. "I'm sure she got here as fast as she could." He pulled out the chair next to him, gestured for Bertie to sit down, and rubbed his hands together. "Now that we're all here, perhaps we should take a minute to compose ourselves before we proceed."

"An excellent idea," Chancellor Grant said. "Can I offer anyone a cup of coffee?"

As Bertie took her seat, she noticed a plus-sized woman sitting at the opposite end of the table. The woman wore a severe black suit, red lipstick, and a scowl.

"What do you think this is, Grant . . . a tea party?" The woman's voice reminded Bertie of a buzz saw. "Quit waltzing around and get down to business."

Terrance Witherspoon coughed discreetly. "Professor Bigelow, this is Mrs. Fania Jones."

Melissa's mother fixed Bertie with a pugnacious glare. "So you're the she-devil who threw my daughter out of choir practice."

Groaning inwardly, Bertie nodded. With her overbearing manner and sarcastic delivery, Melissa's mother reminded Bertie of Aunt Esther from the TV sitcom *Sanford and Son.* Except that this "Aunt Esther" articulated every syllable as though speaking to a room full of mentally challenged three year olds.

"There's no need for unpleasantness, Mrs. Jones," Chancellor Grant said, spreading his hands in a placating gesture. "Surely this matter can be resolved amicably."

"I'm an attorney," Mrs. Jones snapped. "I win arguments for a living. I couldn't care less whether this matter is resolved amicably, as long as it is resolved in my favor." As the chancellor opened his mouth to reply, Mrs. Jones held up her hand. "Let's cut to the chase, shall we?"

The chancellor nodded glumly. If there was one thing Humbert X. Grant hated, it was controversy.

"You people have a problem with the fact that my daughter sent The Ace of Spades a text message. Is this correct?"

"A text message filled with inappropriate content," Bertie said tartly. She was not about to let this maltempered mountain of a woman intimidate her.

"Appropriateness is in the eye of the beholder," Mrs. Jones said. "The man on the receiving end of the messages had no complaints."

I'll bet he didn't, Bertie thought. "Your daughter sent naked pictures of herself to the guest artist for our upcoming concert," Bertie said. "Doesn't this bother you? She even bragged about it to the other students."

"This is a man's world, Mrs. Bigelow. You, of all people, should know that. Having a good body is a huge asset in this business. There's a lot of competition out there. My daughter was merely making the most of her natural abilities."

"We no longer live in the nineteen-fifties," Bertie said, shaking her head in frustration. "It's a new century, for crying out loud. Melissa is talented and intelligent. Don't you think she could have gotten the part without resorting to nudity?"

"What I *think*, Professor, is that Metro College has violated my daughter's right to free speech. What's more, you have grossly overstepped your authority."

Bertie crossed her arms in front of her chest and glowered. "No one has a right to disrupt my classroom, Mrs. Jones."

"C'mon, folks," Terrance Witherspoon said. In spite of the obvious tension in the room, his delivery was as relaxed as a summer Sunday. "Let's dial it back a notch, shall we? Mrs. Jones just wants to see her little girl up there singing and dancing her heart out. Isn't that right?"

Fania Jones grunted in assent.

"And Professor Bigelow just wants to make sure her authority in the classroom is respected," Witherspoon said. "Am I right, Bertie?"

Bertie nodded grimly.

"Now that it's clear what everyone wants, I am sure we can work out a win-win solution." Witherspoon leaned back in his chair, stretched his long legs in front of him, and stared at the ceiling.

"I've got it," he said suddenly. "Melissa will be allowed to participate fully in all Metro Choir activities—"

"That's more like it," Mrs. Jones said, shooting a smug look in Bertie's direction.

"If, and *only* if, she apologizes to her classmates and to Professor Bigelow for the disruption she has caused."

Fania Jones sucked her teeth and rocked back and forth in her chair—an oversized cobra preparing to strike. "That's ridiculous! What's more, it's illegal, coercive, and blatantly unconstitutional."

"Then sue us, Mrs. Jones," Chancellor Grant said sharply. Bertie's boss hated controversy with a purple passion, but he disliked being bullied even more. "Metro College is an educational institution, not a strip club. I will not have students behaving in a lewd and lascivious manner on campus."

"Melissa was not on campus," Mrs. Jones fired back. "What's more, she is over eighteen. Once she leaves this building, she has the legal right to send whatever she wishes to whomever she wishes, whenever she wishes."

"Nonetheless, I have made up my mind," Chancellor Grant said. "If your daughter wishes to participate in this concert, she has exactly one week to apologize. And if she ever engages in this kind of conduct again, she will be expelled."

"In that case, I will see you in court," Mrs. Jones said coolly. With a curt nod, she picked up her briefcase and stalked out of the room.

After a moment of silence, the chancellor sighed heavily. "Guess I'd better put a call in to Abraham & Abraham. Find out whether this woman has a case or not."

When Chancellor Grant had left the room, Terrance Witherspoon shook his head ruefully. "My Lord, what a morning," he said. "The rest of the day has got to be an improvement."

Taking a quick peek to make sure her boss was out of earshot, Bertie took a deep breath and began to sing:

> *My Lord, what a morning*
> *My Lord, what a morning*
> *My Lord, what a morning*
> *When the stars begin to fall.*

"That song is one of my favorite spirituals," she said. "It's about the Last Judgment, you know."

Witherspoon smiled. "This morning was bad, but it wasn't *that* bad." He squeezed Bertie lightly on the arm. "I like the way you handled this situation. You've got a nice way about yourself."

"Thanks," Bertie said. "But you're the one with the people skills. You even got that horrible woman to stop yelling for a few seconds."

"Would have been better if I'd gotten her to stay that way a bit longer," Witherspoon said wryly. His laugh reminded Bertie of the caramel sauce she'd poured over her ice cream as a child. All of a sudden she was very, *very* aware that Terrance Witherspoon was still holding on to her arm.

"Call me if you run into any more trouble," Witherspoon said and stood up. "In fact, call me any time, Bertie. I have a feeling we've got a lot to talk about."

On the way the back to her office, Bertie turned Witherspoon's words over and over in her mind. *Call me any time*, he'd said. Had Terrance Witherspoon just made a pass at her?

Chapter Ten

WEDNESDAY, OCTOBER 18—7:00 PM

Bertie was bone tired by the time she got home from work that evening. As she popped a Lean Cuisine chicken dinner into the microwave and prepared to sink into the soft embrace of her living room
couch, she suddenly realized she'd forgotten to call Charley Howard.
At that moment, the last thing Bertie needed was another high-volt-
age conversation. Still, she had promised Charley she'd report back
after she had seen Sister Destina. Knowing how worried he was about
his wife, it didn't seem right to make him sit on pins and needles waiting for her call. With a weary sigh, Bertie pulled out her phone and
punched in his number.

As she described the details of her visit to the psychic's home, the
Hot Sauce King listened without comment. When she had finished
her report, he chuckled softly.

"Just what I thought, Bertie. Broad's a friggin' phony."

"Most likely," Bertie said. "But she did tell me some things."

"What kind of things?"

"Private things, actually." She was glad Charley could not see her
blushing. "I'd rather not say, if you don't mind."

"Suit yourself. Based on what you've told me, there's not a doubt
in my mind. Sister Destina is a fake. Problem is, Mabel will probably
divorce me if I call the bunko squad."

"How is she, Charley? She hasn't returned my calls."

"Mabel isn't returning anyone's calls," Charley said softly. "Mopes around the house all day. When I ask what's wrong, she looks right through me."

"Mabel needs to get her mind off this thing," Bertie said. "The Ace of Spades is coming to rehearse with my choir on Friday. Do you think she'd like me to get her a backstage pass?"

"Is that the guy who sings 'Be Positive'? Mabel's crazy about him. If he can't cheer her up, nothing will."

Bertie hung up the phone and left Mabel a message. Then, exhausted but somewhat pleased with herself, she popped a bowl of popcorn and stretched out on the couch to watch TV.

When she finally crawled into bed, however, Bertie was unable to sleep. Was Sister Destina really a fraud? It seemed likely, but then what about her prediction regarding the men in Bertie's life? Visions of strolling hand in hand with her "new friend" Denzel Washington whirled through Bertie's mind, alternating with images of having to testify in court. Could Fania Jones really sue the college because Melissa had been kicked out of the choir?

After a frustrating hour spent tossing and turning, Bertie rolled out of bed. As far as she could tell, there was nothing she could do to ascertain the truth of Destina's prediction except to wait and see what happened next. But Melissa's mother was another matter.

David Mackenzie had worked as a Cook County prosecutor before opening his lucrative private practice. In addition, Mackenzie was a close friend—full of optimism, good will, and boundless energy. Surely he would be able to put her mind at ease regarding the litigious Fania Jones.

She picked up her phone and tapped out a text message:

Hey, Mac. It's Bertie. Please call when you get a minute.

Bertie heaved a sigh of relief and crawled back under the covers. When her phone rang an hour later, it woke her from a sound sleep.

"I didn't realize how late it was," David Mackenzie said. "Should I call back tomorrow?"

46

"That's okay, Mac." Rubbing her eyes, Bertie sat up and pulled the covers around her. "I've run into a bit of a legal problem at work. I was hoping you could tell me what to do."

When she mentioned that her problem involved Fania Jones, Mac burst out laughing.

"That ambulance chaser wouldn't know a constitutional issue if it jumped up and smacked her in the face," he said. "But she's right about one thing. Sexting between consenting adults is perfectly legal."

"So she could actually sue the college?"

"She could," Mac admitted. "But it's not likely she'd get very far. As long as you could prove that Melissa was disrupting your classroom, you'd be home free."

"Thanks, Mac." Bertie stifled a yawn. "It was really sweet of you to call me back right away."

"I woke you up, didn't I?" he said sheepishly. "Sorry about that. I haven't been quite myself since Angelique left."

Suddenly, Bertie was no longer sleepy. She threw off the covers and sat on the edge of the bed.

"What do you mean *since Angelique left?*"

Angelique Mackenzie had never been high on Bertie's list of favorite people. The woman had an inferiority complex the size of Texas and a mouth to match. Though she'd never said so, Bertie had always felt Mac was way too good for her.

"Angie's been seeing someone else for months. I'm surprised you didn't know. Everyone else did. Everyone but me, that is."

"How awful for you," Bertie said softly. "How are you coping?"

"Okay, I suppose. Been nursing my wounds since she moved out six weeks ago."

"I know what it's like to find yourself alone in an empty house," Bertie said. "If you need a shoulder to cry on, call me."

"Thanks," Mackenzie said. After a pause, he added softly, "You have no idea how much that means to me."

Chapter Eleven

THURSDAY, OCTOBER 19—7:00 AM

When her alarm went off at seven the next morning, Bertie was tempted to ignore it and sleep for another hour. Her life had been crazy for the past five days. Charley's restaurant had been hexed. Melissa's mother had threatened to sue her. And now, on top of everything else, David and Angelique Mackenzie were breaking up. Bertie craved a drama-free day more than anything—twenty-four mundane hours where absolutely nothing out of the ordinary occurred.

But today was not going to be that day.

Today, Sam Willis, a.k.a. The Ace of Spades, was flying in from LA to rehearse with the Metro College Singers. And today, Bertie Bigelow was going to pick him up at the airport. To add to the drama, Hedda Eberhardt had informed her late yesterday afternoon that The Ace would be not be flying into nearby Midway Airport. Instead, he would be arriving at O'Hare International Airport, a forty-mile round trip from Bertie's South Side home.

Ellen Simpson had offered to act as a chaperone during the long trip. "That man is sexual dynamite, Bertie. You sure you can handle him all by yourself?"

"Our relationship is strictly professional," Bertie told her. "I don't intend to flirt, and I don't intend to fawn over him either."

"Don't you read *People* magazine? The Ace has got a serious reputation where women are concerned. His former backup singer is suing him for child support right now."

"Come on, Ellen. What's he going to do? Molest me on the way home from the airport?"

"You never know," Ellen said darkly. "And I'm not necessarily saying it would be a bad thing if he did. But if he does make a play, you want to be in complete control, if you get my drift." She extracted a small black canister from her handbag and placed it in Bertie's hand. "Here. Take my pepper spray. Just in case."

Although Bertie had dutifully placed the canister in her purse, she felt confident that everything was going to turn out just fine. Though she hadn't wanted to make a big deal out of it, she was a huge fan of The Ace's 2004 hit song "Be Positive."

Dressed with casual elegance in a tight-fitting pair of Calvin Klein jeans, knee-high boots, and a gray cashmere turtleneck, Bertie hummed a few bars of the tune while checking her reflection in the mirror. Its catchy melody put Bertie in such a good mood that she continued to sing as she walked outside.

> No matter what you're goin' through
> Be positive. Keep it positive.
> Life is tough, but so are you.
> Be positive. Keep it positive.

As she warbled her way down the driveway, Pat O'Fallon called to her from the other side of the fence.

"Top o' the mornin' to ya, Bertie."

As Bertie waved back, she smiled to herself. When she was a child, almost all of Chicago's neighborhoods had been segregated. Never in her wildest dreams had she imagined she would one day live next door to a pair of Irish ladies. But things had changed. If not everywhere, at least in Bertie's tiny corner of the city. Pat O'Fallon and her sister Colleen were retired teachers who looked to be in their early eighties. Small and frail, the two sisters sported identical halos of wispy white hair and watery blue eyes that did not miss a trick.

"Is that Bertie?" Colleen said, poking her head out the front window.

"The very same," Pat said. "Sportin' a pair of skintight jeans and singin' to beat the band."

"Where ya off to, Bertie?" Dressed in a faded gingham housedress and a pair of run-down mules, Colleen stepped onto her front porch to have a better look. "Must be somethin' grand to get ya singin' at this hour."

Striking identical poses with their hands on their hips and their heads cocked to the left, the O'Fallon sisters waited expectantly. Unless Bertie was prepared to be outright rude, she would not be able to leave the driveway until she told the sisters where she was going.

"I'm on my way out to O'Hare to pick up The Ace of Spades," Bertie said. "You've probably never heard of him, but he's a famous singer."

Colleen O'Fallon clapped her hands in excitement. "The boy who sings 'Be Positive'?"

"Of course," Pat said, shooting her sister a derogatory glare. "Why else would Bertie be singin' his song?"

"You don't have to snap at me," Colleen said. "I was just tryin' ta make sure."

Pat O'Fallon snorted. "Ya was hornin' in on the conversation. Just like ya always do."

Bertie sighed inwardly. As far as she could tell, Pat and Colleen O'Fallon had been having the same argument every day for as long as she'd known them. Stealing a quick glance at her watch, Bertie decided to change the subject.

"I didn't know you ladies liked pop music," she said.

"Are you kidding?" Pat said. "A course we do." She began to sing in a high, reedy voice: "Be positive, whoa whoa. Positive."

"Keep it positive," Colleen chimed in. "The Ace is tops in my book, Bertie. Be sure to bring us back an autograph."

The traffic on the Dan Ryan Expressway was terrible. Despite the fair weather outside, Bertie rolled up the window of her Honda in a vain attempt to shut out the noise and fumes from the fourteen lanes of traffic crawling toward the center of the city. After inching at an agonizing pace past the downtown skyscrapers, Bertie got stuck for thirty minutes behind a large tractor-trailer waiting to merge onto I-290.

By the time she parked her car in the garage and sprinted for what seemed like ten miles to the baggage claim area, Bertie was nearly an hour late. If she'd had The Ace's cell number, she could have called. But for some reason, Hedda Eberhardt had neglected to give it to her.

A large white man stopped her as she ran toward the baggage carousel.

"You Bigelow?" he said curtly.

Tall and heavily muscled, his arms were covered with tattoos. Silver rings hung from his nose and both earlobes.

Bertie nodded glumly.

"About freakin' time," the man snapped. "I *told* Ace we should have chartered a limo." He turned his back on Bertie and hollered: "Yo, Ace. Our ride's here. Finally."

As The Ace of Spades approached them, he looked older than Bertie had imagined. He wore a nondescript black T-shirt, wrinkled jeans, and a pair of unlaced Timberlands. The sultry bedroom eyes, for which he was famous, were hidden behind a pair of dark aviator glasses, and his trademark curls had been stuffed under a White

Sox baseball cap. A small potbelly protruded above the waistband of his jeans.

"I'm Sam Willis, otherwise known as The Ace of Spades," he said. He grinned and stuck out his hand. "This here's Bulldog, my chief of security."

"Sorry about being late," Bertie said as she shook his hand. "The traffic was terrible."

"Water under the bridge, Mrs. Bigelow. Never worry about the things you can't change." The Ace turned to Bulldog and pointed to the jumble of suitcases scattered at his feet. "I'm gonna go straight to my mama's place. Make sure my stuff gets to the hotel in one piece."

"Maybe I should come with you," Bulldog said. "You remember what happened in Detroit when you went off on your own."

"Yeah, but that was Motown. I'm on my home turf now. Anyway, nobody's gonna recognize me in this raggedy get-up." Without another word, The Ace ambled off in the direction of the parking garage.

The Dan Ryan was even more crowded than it had been an hour ago. However, The Ace didn't seem to mind. The singer stared pensively at the passing scenery as Bertie piloted her Honda through the massive snarl of traffic.

"Chi-town," he said softly. "Fifteen years ago, I never thought I'd make it out of here."

"It must feel good to know how far you've come," Bertie said.

"I s'pose," The Ace said. "My mama taught math at Englewood High back in the day. Bet you didn't know that."

"Actually, I did," Bertie said. "I've been following your career for years."

The Ace shrugged dismissively and continued staring out the window. "If I got below ninety on a test, Mama would whup my behind.

To this day, I can tell you all the prime numbers up to one hundred."

"I know what you mean," Bertie said with a smile. "I was not allowed to leave the house until Dad checked over my homework. Sounds pretty corny, but that's how it was."

"Corny is good sometimes," The Ace said. "My mama didn't take no stuff. She was a great teacher too. Always pushed me to do my best."

"Clearly, it worked," Bertie said. "You're Metro's most famous graduate—a role model for thousands of kids. My students are beyond thrilled to be performing with you." She paused. "One of them may have gotten a little *too* thrilled, if you catch my drift."

The Ace burst out laughing. "I think I know where you're going with this one, Mrs. Bigelow."

"I don't want to sound like a prude or anything, but this whole sexting business has put my classroom in an uproar." Bertie hadn't planned to discuss the incident, but now that she'd started, she was determined to get her point across. "The word on campus is that Melissa only got to dance in the show because of the naked pictures she sent."

The Ace turned away from the window and leaned forward. "I've been on the road for fifteen years, Mrs. Bigelow. After 'Be Positive' came out, girls used to line up outside my hotel room every night. Things got so crazy, Bulldog had to guard my door so I could get some privacy."

"So you didn't give Melissa a bigger part in the show because she sexted you?"

The Ace grunted. "I'm a professional, Mrs. Bigelow. You think I'd jeopardize the quality of my show over a pair of tits? I chose Melissa because of the YouTube clip she sent me of her dancing to 'Be Positive.' The girl's got some really nice moves."

Bertie smiled. "If you could take a minute before tomorrow's rehearsal to repeat what you just said to my choir, it would solve a lot of problems."

"I'd be glad to, Mrs. Bigelow," The Ace said.

"Call me Bertie. Mrs. Bigelow makes me feel like an old lady."

"You sure don't look like one," he said. "Say, listen, you've been so nice, picking me up and driving me around like this. Why don't you join me and my mama for lunch? She's hardly left the house since she had her heart attack last month. I know she'd love to talk shop with another teacher."

"Wish I could," Bertie said, "but I've got to teach this afternoon. Thanks for the offer, though."

"Some other time?"

"Oh, you don't have to do that," Bertie said, hoping The Ace hadn't noticed the sudden flush in her cheeks. "I know you're busy."

"Never too busy for pleasant conversation," he said. "I like you, Bertie. Next time I'm in town, I'm not gonna take no for an answer."

Ten minutes later, Bertie pulled onto Throop Street and parked in front of a small brick house in the middle of the block.

"I've been all over the world—Rome, Paris, LA, you name it," the singer said. "But I was born and raised in Englewood. And when the time comes for me to settle down, I'm gonna come right back." Flashing his trademark grin, The Ace stepped out of the car. "Like Diana Ross says in *The Wiz*, there's no place like home."

As she piloted her car eastward along Seventy-First Street past a vacant lot and a row of boarded-up buildings, Bertie found herself smiling despite the bleakness of her surroundings. The airport pick-up had gotten off on the wrong foot. But in the end, things had not turned out too badly. It was a relief to learn that The Ace was not as difficult as she'd feared. Despite his reputation as a womanizer, the man seemed thoughtful and intelligent. Not to mention that sexy smile of his.

Wait till I tell Ellen he asked me to his mama's house for lunch. And Mabel Howard? The poor thing is going to be green with envy.

In the midst of this pleasant reverie, it suddenly occurred to Bertie that Mabel had not actually confirmed that she would be coming to the workshop. In order to meet The Ace in person, Mabel was going to need to pick up a backstage pass. Bertie flipped on her turn signal, pulled her Honda to the curb, and punched Mabel's number into her cell phone.

"Hey, Bertie," Mabel said and sighed glumly.

"Did I catch you at a bad time?" Bertie said. "I have something exciting to tell you, but I can call back later."

"Might as well tell me now and get it over with."

"You okay? You sound depressed."

"I am most definitely NOT okay," Mabel replied with sudden vigor. "I've been duped. Punk'd. Taken advantage of. What's worse, I've dragged my husband's business into the mud."

"You talking about Sister Destina?"

"Who else?" Mabel said bitterly. "There was never a hex on Charley's restaurant. Commissioner Jefferson got sick because Destina paid someone to sprinkle rotten meat in his food."

"Are you sure?" Bertie said. She had never heard her friend so angry.

"Of course I'm sure," Mabel said sharply. "I went by Destina's house this morning. I didn't have an appointment, but I figured maybe, if I got there early enough, she'd be able to squeeze me in. While I'm sitting in the waiting room, I can hear her talking to someone on the phone. 'You used too damn much of that spoiled ham hock I gave you,' she says. 'Almost killed the commissioner.' Then she laughs. 'We sho' nuff settled Charley Howard's hash. That simple-ass wife of his is gonna think I walk on water.'

"I suppose I should have confronted Destina," Mabel said. "But I was too shocked to think straight. The only thing I wanted to do was get out of there. I tiptoed out the front door, got in my car, and drove away."

"Poor thing," Bertie said. "Bet Charley blew his stack when you told him."

"I didn't tell him," Mabel said sharply. "And I don't want you telling him either. Ever since we've been married, Charley's been looking after me, taking care of me. It's about time I handled my own business, Bertie. I'm getting my money back from that phony psychic if it's the last damn thing I do."

"You should go to the police," Bertie said. "Sister Destina probably has a rap sheet as long as your arm."

"No need for that," Mabel said. "I've got a plan."

"What kind of plan?"

"That, my friend, is top secret."

"Please don't tell me you're arranging some kind of confrontation," Bertie said. "If what you're saying is true, Sister Destina has already tried to poison somebody. You don't want to get yourself hurt."

"You worry too much," Mabel said. "I refuse to waste another minute talking about this foolishness."

"Come on, Mabel. Can't you at least give me a hint about this plan of yours?"

"Leave it alone, girlfriend." The edge in Mabel's voice took Bertie by surprise.

"In that case, let me tell you why I called," Bertie said in a lighter tone.

By the time she was finished telling Mabel about her morning's adventures, her friend's customary good nature had begun to return.

"Did you know The Ace is a Scorpio?" Mabel said. "That's a water sign, you know—very intense. He was born on the same day as Drake. Drake is my absolute favorite rapper. Kinda figures, doesn't it. Great artists tend to come from the fixed signs. That's where they get their power. But there I go again, rambling on. Charley used to say I had a mind like a sieve, except for birthdays. I never forget a birthday." After a nervous giggle, Mabel's voice turned serious. "Just do me one favor, okay?"

"Anything," Bertie said. "What do you need?"

"I know Charley's paying you to investigate Sister Destina. I don't even mind 'cause I know he's been worried about me, poor thing. But please. Don't say anything to Charley about this. At least not until tomorrow. Can you promise me that?"

"As long as you promise not to do anything rash," Bertie said firmly. "Promise you won't go off half-cocked on this thing."

"Don't worry, Bertie. What I'm planning is completely legal. I'll tell you all about it tomorrow when I see you."

"It's a deal," Bertie said. "I'll leave your backstage pass at the box office. See you after the show."

Bertie kept her students at rehearsal until nearly eight o'clock that evening. She was determined to do whatever it took to make sure the choir's performance at the next day's rehearsal was as strong as possible. In her quest for perfection, she spared no one. By the time practice was over, both she and her students were exhausted.

When she finally got home that night, Bertie nuked a Weight Watchers veggie pizza in the microwave, poured herself a glass of Merlot, and watched a parade of meaningless TV programs until midnight.

Chapter Twelve

Friday, October 20—5:50 AM

When Bertie's cell phone rang the next morning at five fifty a.m., she thought it was part of her dream. Melissa Jones had been tap dancing naked down a golden staircase while the choir, dressed for some strange reason entirely in polka-dot pajamas, sang the chorus from "Pennies from Heaven." In a tinny voice, Marvin Gaye kept repeating the same insistent phrase: "What's Goin' On, What's Goin' On, What's . . ."

Bertie grabbed the phone off her night table and mumbled a groggy hello.

"It's Sister Destina," the psychic said in her husky baritone. "Please don't hang up."

"Give me one good reason not to. First of all, it is not even six o'clock in the morning. Second, I know all about your sleazy little scam."

"That's why I'm calling you," Sister Destina said, her voice beginning to tremble. "I want to clear my karma. To atone before it's too late."

"You should have thought about your karma before you started ripping people off," Bertie said tartly.

"I admit I've done some terrible things, Bertie. And yes, I paid one of the commissioner's interns to put rotten meat in his dinner. But please. Give me a chance to explain."

"Why should I? Your phony prophecies have caused a lot of damage."

"They're not entirely fake," Sister Destina said softly, then paused for a moment. "Met any interesting men lately?"

Bertie was silent. Between Terrance Witherspoon giving her the eye, The Ace asking her to meet his mama, and David Mackenzie calling in the middle of the night, she'd gotten more attention from men in the past two days then she'd had in the past year.

Sister Destina chuckled. "I told you there'd be three new men in your life. Which one came on to you yesterday, Bertie? Was it the old friend? The new friend? I sure hope it wasn't the false friend."

"Stop talking nonsense," Bertie said. "If you were a real psychic, you wouldn't be out there scamming people."

"That's what I'm trying to tell you," Sister Destina said urgently. "It's not what you think."

"Why me, Destina? We barely know each other."

"My spirit guides say you are the only person who can help me. Come to my house tonight. I promise I'll explain everything. It's a matter of life and death," the psychic said and hung up.

Bertie sighed. Unlike Destina's phony fortune-telling act, the terror and desperation in the psychic's voice had been real. Of that, Bertie was certain. The psychic had run out of options and was about to suffer the inevitable consequences of her behavior. And although Bertie felt a small pang of sympathy for Destina's predicament, she had more important things on her mind. At four o'clock today, after months of preparation, her students were going to perform onstage with The Ace of Spades. True, it was only a workshop and not the final performance. But still.

Bertie made a mental checklist of dos and don'ts for the day:

- ✓ Make sure The Ace has bottled water and fresh fruit in his dressing room.
- ✓ Remember to invite Dr. Grant and Terrance Witherspoon backstage.

- ✓ Remember to spend extra time warming up the alto section.
- ✓ Move on from the sexting incident. Tactfully remind The Ace to explain his reasons for choosing Melissa's dance number.
- ✓ Reserve a seat in the front row for Mabel Howard.
- ✓ Take three deep breaths before going onstage.
- ✓ Stay focused. Don't think about anything else but the job at hand.

"And above all," Bertie said to herself as she threaded her Honda through the traffic on Halsted Street, "be positive. It's going to be a great day."

The Metro College Performance Center was filled by the time Bertie's students arrived. Bursting with nervous energy and turned out in their Sunday best, they milled restlessly around the auditorium. As Bertie corralled her choir in the dressing room backstage, they peppered her with questions.

"Have you seen The Ace?"

"What's he like? Is he nice?"

"Where is he? Shouldn't he be here by now? You sure he's coming?"

"Quiet, everyone," Bertie said. "Let's get warmed up so we'll be ready to go when he gets here."

Melissa Jones remained conspicuously absent. When Bertie asked if anyone had seen the girl, Nyala Clark shook her head.

"She hasn't been to any of her classes this week," Nyala said. "Word is, her mother's keeping her out of school till the court case is settled."

"Court case?" Maurice Green said sharply. "What court case?"

"Where you been, fool?" Nyala said, giving Maurice a pitying look. "Melissa's mama is gonna sue the college for throwing her out of the choir."

Bertie held up her hand for silence. "Now hold on one moment, Nyala. No one knows for certain exactly what Melissa's mother is going to do. I have not received any official notification from the chancellor. In fact, I'm still hoping Melissa will do the right thing—apologize for her behavior and return to the choir."

Nyala's skeptical expression was mirrored on the faces of her classmates. "With all due respect, Mrs. B, I don't see that happening. Today's workshop is the biggest thing our choir has ever done. And Melissa didn't even bother to show up."

"Why don't you let me worry about that," Bertie said, projecting what she hoped was a cheerful lack of concern. "We'll cut Melissa's number for now. After the workshop, I'll ask the dean of students to find out what is going on. Right now, we've got more important things to worry about." She sat down on the piano bench and plunked out an authoritative chord. "Arpeggios, ladies and gentlemen, on my downbeat."

As the students continued to warm up their voices, Bertie stared anxiously at the clock on the wall in front of her. The Ace should have arrived an hour ago. If the singer didn't turn up soon, she was going to have some very disappointed students on her hands.

Halfway through her fifth set of vocal exercises, the door to the dressing room burst open. The singing trailed off as the students craned their necks for a better look. Dressed from head to toe in black leather, The Ace of Spades swept into the room.

"Whazzup, Metro?!" he shouted, pumping his fists. His shirt was unbuttoned almost to his navel, and three enormous gold chains sparkled against his bare chest. "Let's make some noise!"

Ten minutes later, the choir had taken their places onstage where The Ace tapped impatiently on a microphone and waved to the soundman in the balcony.

From her place in the wings, Bertie peered out into the auditorium. The house was full. Chancellor Grant and Terrance Witherspoon sat in the front row, while Ellen Simpson, unmistakable in a purple and gold African dress, sat next to Maria Francione in the balcony.

The only person Bertie did not see was Mabel Howard. She was not sitting in the front row seat Bertie had reserved for her. Nor did Mabel appear to be among the latecomers rushing to take their seats in the back of the house. But in that moment, Bertie Bigelow did not have time to worry about Mabel or anything else.

It was showtime.

As the house lights dimmed and the curtain went up, Bertie took three deep breaths, stepped onto the stage, and up to the microphone.

"Thanks for waiting, everyone," she said. "Before we begin, I'd like to take a moment to introduce the clinician for today's workshop. Sam Willis, known to you as The Ace of Spades, grew up on the South Side of Chicago and attended Metro Community College, or Metro Junior College, as it was known in those days. In 2000, Mr. Willis signed a contract with Tone Def Records and moved to Los Angeles. And in 2004, he wrote his chart-topping song 'Be Positive.' The rest, as they say, is history."

"Yo, Ace," a female voice sang out in the darkness. "We love you!"

When the whistling and clapping had died down, Bertie continued. "What you are about to see is a workshop. Mr. Willis will be stopping the choir frequently to make corrections and to share his musical expertise. To repeat, this is a workshop, not a performance, so please bear with us. Finally, I will ask that you turn off your cell phones. Anyone caught recording or photographing The Ace without his permission will be asked to leave the auditorium."

Bulldog, The Ace's bodyguard, stepped up to the edge of the stage and surveyed the crowd menacingly.

"Listen up," he shouted. "I catch you recording the show today, I will personally throw both you and your phone outta here. Got it?"

For the next two hours, Bertie watched appreciatively as The Ace of Spades put the Metro College Singers through their paces. Once in front of the students, the singer shed his laid-back demeanor. He stopped the group frequently and made corrections in a crisp, no-nonsense manner. Fascinated, the audience hung on every word.

"Never forget that music is a discipline," The Ace said, shaking his finger at the alto section. "It isn't enough just to sing your heart out. You gotta work at it every single day. Y'all need to work on your intonation here. It's out of tune because you are not supporting your notes. Bet Mrs. Bigelow has told you that a million times."

"Yeah," Nyala Clark said sheepishly. "When you come back next time, we're gonna have it. You'll see."

The Ace nodded. "You better. I am not getting up on stage with a bunch of raggedy-ass amateurs." The students stared, crestfallen, at the floor until The Ace waved his hand dismissively. "Based on what you've shown me today, I know you guys are capable. You work hard for the next three weeks, and we are gonna have one hell of a show."

At the end of the rehearsal, Bulldog stood guard as a crowd of eager students clustered around The Ace, snapping photos and asking him for autographs. When the final "#selfiew/Ace" had been taken, Bertie shook the singer's hand warmly.

"Thanks again for doing this," she said. "It has meant the world to my students."

"My pleasure," he said. He bent down and kissed her gently on the cheek. "When I come back next time, I want you to meet my mama. No excuses, all right?"

Bertie turned beet red. As she fumbled for a reply, Bulldog walked toward them and tapped The Ace on the shoulder.

"Time to go," he said. "Our show in Gary starts at eight. The limo's waiting."

Long after The Ace had said goodbye, the students milled around the stage, excitedly reviewing the day's events. Even Chancellor Grant was pleased.

"Congratulations, Professor Bigelow," he said. "Your students did a fine job." Lowering his voice, he took a step closer. "I notice Melissa Jones didn't sing with the group. Have you heard from her?"

"Not a peep," Bertie said.

"Oh dear. I suppose I'd better have Dr. Witherspoon give her mother a call." As the chancellor turned away, Ellen rushed onstage to give Bertie a hug.

"The Ace may be a bit fatter than he was ten years ago," she said. "But my, oh my, that man is *fine*."

"Don't I know it," Bertie said. "He kissed me. Right here on the cheek. Told me he wants to introduce me to his mama the next time he's in town."

Ellen grinned. "Bet he uses that line at least ten times a day. Still. If he makes a serious play for you, I want to be the first to know."

"Girl, you are too crazy," Bertie said, laughing. "By the way, have you seen Mabel Howard? We were supposed to meet up after the show."

"Nope. Maybe she had to leave early or something. If I see her, I'll tell her you're looking for her."

By this point, the auditorium was nearly empty. Mabel had promised to meet her after the rehearsal, and it was not like Mabel to break a promise. Bertie checked her phone for messages. Nothing. Worse still, Mabel was not answering her cell phone.

It had been a long and event-filled day, and now that it was nearly over, Bertie was ready to go home and put her feet up. Whatever was going on with Mabel Howard would just have to wait until the next day.

Bertie was halfway home when she remembered her conversation with Sister Destina that morning. The psychic had asked her to stop by, but it had been a long day. In Bertie's mind nothing Destina could say could possibly justify the way she'd treated Mabel Howard. Which led Bertie to wonder, not for the first time, where Mabel was. Why hadn't she shown up for The Ace's clinic? Mabel had been hopping mad the last time they'd spoken—furious, in fact. Could she have ignored Bertie's advice and taken matters into her own hands?

As Bertie approached the corner of Sixty-Third and Cottage Grove, she had an unsettling thought. *Mabel Howard could very well be sitting in Destina's living room at this very moment.*

Heaving a sigh, Bertie made a U-turn in the middle of Sixty-Third Street and headed back toward the Dan Ryan Expressway.

Chapter Thirteen

FRIDAY, OCTOBER 20—8:00 PM

Music blared through Sister Destina's open window as Bertie pulled her car to the curb. Certainly, it was not unusual to hear loud music wafting through open windows in Morgan Park. Not at all. But instead of Nicki Minaj, Kanye West, or Jay Z, Sister Destina was listening to the blues. Accompanied by the old-fashioned beat of an out-of-tune ragtime piano, Bessie Smith's voice was unmistakable:

> Gee, but it's hard to love someone
> When that someone don't love you.
> I'm so disgusted,
> Heartbroken, too . . .

It seemed an odd choice for background music. Odder still was the fact that Sister Destina had left her front door wide open.

After knocking and calling out a tentative "hello," Bertie stepped inside. The music was so loud it hurt:

> Trouble, trouble, I've had it all my days.
> Trouble, trouble, I've had it all my days.
> Seem like trouble's goin' to follow me to my grave.

No wonder Destina can't hear me, Bertie thought. *I can barely hear myself.*

Stuffing her fingers in her ears, she took a look around. The waiting room was empty, and every light in the place had been turned on. Deprived of its usual dim lighting, the room looked distinctly tacky. There were cracks in the walls and a water stain on the ceiling. Destina's pink velvet sofa was shiny from overuse, and even the velvet Jesus hanging on the far wall looked like he'd seen better days.

"Destina, it's me—Bertie Bigelow. Are you in there?"

The door to Destina's inner sanctum had also been left ajar. Bertie pushed it open and walked inside as Bessie Smith's gritty lament continued to pour at top volume from an oversized boom box in the corner:

> *You mistreated me and drove me from your door.*
> *Mistreated me and drove me from your door.*
> *But the Good Book says you'll reap just what you sow.*

The spotlights over the psychic's throne had been turned on full. Harsh beams of brilliant white light bounced off the glossy white walls and careened off the glossy white furniture.

Sister Destina lay sprawled on the floor with her head tilted at an impossible angle. Blood spattered the ceiling above her, stained the wall behind her throne, and dripped onto the glossy white floor. Her white wedding dress was torn and streaked with crimson. The ceremonial sword Destina had once brandished to chase away demons now protruded from her enormous stomach.

Bertie stood frozen in disbelief for several seconds as her mind struggled desperately to comprehend the scene before her. Then she began to scream. As she ran out of the house, Bessie Smith's voice followed her:

> *Trouble, trouble, I've had it all my days.*
> *Trouble, trouble, gonna follow me to my grave.*

Outside on the sidewalk, Bertie Bigelow took a deep breath, dug out her cell phone with shaking fingers, and called 911.

For the next few hours, a small army of policemen streamed in and out of Sister Destina's inner sanctum, photographing the body and dusting for fingerprints. As Bertie sat numbly in the psychic's shabby waiting room, Detective Michael Kulicki arrived, accompanied by his partner, a gangly black man with a cauliflower ear and a sullen expression. Although Bertie had met Kulicki during her investigation into the murder of Judge Theophilous Green, the detective did not seem pleased to see her. Haggard, as always, with a smoker's cough and a jaw lined with five-o'clock shadow, Kulicki immediately began to pepper her with questions.

What was her connection to Sister Destina? Why had she come to visit the psychic that evening? Had she seen or heard anyone inside the house?

"Sister Destina asked me to come by here tonight," Bertie said. "She had something important to show me."

"Something important? Like what, Mrs. Bigelow?"

Bertie shook her head. "Honestly, I have no idea. Maybe her assistant would know."

Kulicki's partner pulled a ballpoint pen and a small notebook out of his back pocket. Slowly, as if speaking through a dense fog, Bertie spelled out Jabarion Coutze's name and gave the police his description.

"Did Sister Destina have any enemies?"

Again, Bertie shook her head. "I really couldn't say. I guess you could try asking her regular clients."

Detective Kulicki grunted. "And were you?"

"Was I what?"

"A regular client." He leaned forward and pinned her with a steely gaze. "What exactly was your relationship with the deceased?"

"It's complicated, I'm afraid. My friend Mabel Howard had been coming here a lot. Her husband asked me to find out if Sister Destina was ripping her off."

"And what did you find out, Mrs. Bigelow? Was Sister Destina a fraud?"

Bertie nodded slowly. All she wanted to do was lie down. Her temples were throbbing, and her eyes ached with fatigue.

"So you lied when you said Destina had no enemies."

Bertie flushed and looked away.

"I'm going to ask you one more time, Mrs. Bigelow. Did you see anyone leaving Sister Destina's house this evening?"

"I already told you," Bertie said. "I didn't see anyone. Am I free to go now?"

"For the moment," Kulicki said tersely. "But don't even think about leaving the city without letting me know."

Chapter Fourteen

The image of Sister Destina sprawled on the floor and covered in blood haunted Bertie's dreams. Who could have done such a horrible thing? Surely there was no way anyone as sweet and gentle as Mabel Howard could be capable of plunging a sword into Destina's belly. Surely not. Mabel was thin, while the psychic had been huge. Yet, something nagged at Bertie's memory. Hadn't Mabel been the captain of the fencing team her senior year at Georgia State University?

Shaking her head clear of these disturbing thoughts, Bertie dragged herself out of bed, staggered into the bathroom, and splashed cold water on her face. What she needed was an activity—something to take her mind off things. For the past week, she'd been meaning to rake up the leaves scattered across her yard. But between preparing for The Ace's workshop and investigating Sister Destina's phony predictions, the task had remained undone. This morning, Bertie decided, she was going to have a clean yard, come hell or high water. *Order in the midst of chaos,* she told herself. Stability in a time of change, not to mention some much-needed fresh air.

Pulling on a Metro College sweatshirt and a pair of tattered jeans, Bertie pried the rake loose from the neglected pile of yard tools in the basement, unfolded an oversized yard waste bag, and stepped outside.

It was another one of those brilliant Indian summer days that make up for the pain of coping with Chicago's harsh winters and scorching summers. As always, when the weather was fair, Bertie was happy she lived near the lake. No matter how hot, stuffy, or stagnant the energy in the western part of the city, if you lived close to Lake Michigan, there was always a breeze. The sun felt warm and welcoming, and fat, puffy clouds floated across a picture-perfect blue sky.

On the other side of the small chain-link fence that separated their yard from Bertie's, the O'Fallon sisters were also doing yard work. While Pat raked leaves into neat multicolored piles, Colleen snipped away at a rogue patch of English Ivy with an oversized pair of garden shears.

"Mornin'," Colleen called out in her reedy Irish brogue. "Grand day, isn't it?"

"I s'pose," Bertie said absently. Normally, the vibrant red of the leaves lying on the ground would have appeared beautiful. Today, they reminded her of blood.

"You *suppose?*" Pat put down her rake and walked over to stand next to her sister by the fence. "Something botherin' ya, Bertie?"

Bertie sighed. "Someone I know was murdered last night." As the two elderly women clucked sympathetically, Bertie recounted the story of her visit to Sister Destina's house. "The worst part is, I was the one to find the body."

Pat reached across the fence and patted Bertie's hand. "Don't let it worry ya, Bertie. Surely, the police will sort the matter out."

"Sure they will," Colleen chimed in. "A good copper always gets his man, or so my cousin Billy used ta say. Isn't that right, Pat?"

"Right as rain," Pat said. "Our Billy was a captain in the fourth precinct for years. Never let a murderer elude him, I can assure you."

Although she kept her expression pleasant, Bertie shuddered inwardly. Her memories of policemen were not those of the friendly Irish cop on the beat. For Bertie, as for many black Chicagoans, the cop on the beat was often anything but friendly. It had been a beefy

Irish policeman, perhaps even Pat O'Fallon's cousin Billy, who'd pulled Bertie's brother out of his car and broken his nose for no particular reason. Although Bertie knew the O'Fallons meant well, there were some things the two sisters would never understand.

As she cast about in her mind for a tactful response, the phone in her kitchen began to ring. Bidding the elderly sisters a hasty goodbye, Bertie ran inside and picked up the receiver.

"Thank God," Charley Howard said. "I was about to hang up and try your cell phone. The cops have taken Mabel down to the station for questioning."

"My Lord." Bertie pulled out a chair and sat down heavily. "She should have a lawyer by her side. Have you called Mac?"

"Of course I've called him," Charley shouted. "Dammit, Bertie! This whole thing is all my fault."

"How can you possibly say that? You did everything you could to get Mabel away from Sister Destina."

"I've been working too much," Charley said. "Spending too many nights at the restaurant. If I'd been around more, Mabel would have never gotten involved with a psychic in the first place."

"Don't worry," Bertie said. "I'm sure she has a perfectly good explanation for her whereabouts on the night of the murder."

The Hot Sauce King grunted. "I hope you're right, Bertie. Thing is, Mabel refuses to talk about it. That's why I need your help. You gotta get her to open up, find out what's really going on."

"Wouldn't you be better off hiring a professional detective? I haven't really done you much good so far."

"Mabel trusts you. That makes you the perfect person for the job."

"Perhaps," Bertie said. "But there's something you need to know. Remember I told you about The Ace's workshop last night? I got Mabel a backstage pass and a front row seat. But she never showed up. I looked all over for her, Charley. She never came."

"Do the police know?"

"I don't think so. The cops didn't ask, and I didn't tell."

Charley Howard sighed. "Let's just keep it that way. And for God's sake, talk some sense into my wife, Bertie. I'm counting on you."

After hanging up the phone, Bertie spent the next several moments brooding. She'd assured Charley that she had not mentioned anything about Mabel to the police. But her memory of the previous night was hazy, at best. She'd been exhausted, disoriented, and terrified. Is it possible she had let something slip?

With a loud sigh, Bertie told herself to cease and desist from idle speculation, at least for the moment. She had a major concert in less than three weeks. She had emails to answer, papers to grade, and a life to live. A life that did not involve Mabel Howard, policemen, psychics, or murder.

Chapter Fifteen

With a determined step, Bertie marched up the stairs, sat down at her bedroom work table, and fired up her computer.

At the top of her email list was a letter from the registrar's office reminding her that Monday was the last day to withdraw students who had stopped coming to class.

Bertie chewed her lip thoughtfully. She had not heard a peep from Melissa Jones since the sexting incident. Should the girl be withdrawn? Bertie leaned back in her swivel chair and stared pensively out the window for several minutes. No, she decided. There was still a chance Melissa would come to her senses and apologize. For the time being, the girl would remain enrolled in the choir.

The doorbell rang as Bertie prepared to read her next email. When she opened the door, a harried UPS man thrust a package into her hands.

As she watched his truck drive away, Bertie shook her head.

That's odd, she thought to herself. She hadn't ordered anything from Amazon and wasn't expecting any packages. It wasn't Christmas, nor was it anywhere near her birthday.

Deep in thought, Bertie closed the door and set the package on the table. Ellen's nemesis, George Frayley, had received a gift-wrapped box of dog poop from a disgruntled student last semester. Could this be a similar prank?

The box was rectangular in shape and weighed about three pounds. If it did contain poop, there was no telltale odor. A more cautious person might have thrown the mysterious package away. But for better and sometimes for worse, Bertie Bigelow had never been a cautious person.

She grabbed a knife from the kitchen drawer and cut away the wrapping paper. Taped to the front of a cardboard shoe box was a single sheet of pink stationary.

> My Dear Bertie,
> When I read your aura yesterday, I knew I could trust you with my masterpiece. I am a psychic, after all. I know these things.
> Hugs,
> Destina

Inside the shoebox was a typewritten manuscript. The title page read:

Toward an Epistemology of Gullibility:
Unpacking the Cultic Milieu of Psychicism
BY
DUSTIN-DESTINA KINGSLEY

Submitted for the degree of Doctor of Philosophy
Department of Psychology
University of Chicago

Of the many things Bertie had anticipated the package might contain, a Ph.D. thesis was definitely not one of them. Shaking her head in amazement, she began to read:

> One in every seven Americans will consult a psychic this year. Who are these people? As a psychologist, I was eager to find out. I set up shop in a lower-class

neighborhood on Chicago's Southwest Side to study this strange phenomenon.

My first order of business was to make sure that the address I used did not contain the number six.

Destina described the house, the neighborhood, and the local atmosphere in excruciating detail. After several pages, the following sentence caught Bertie's eye:

> Mabel H., a thirty-six-year-old African-American female, was the ideal subject for my research. To test the limits of her credulity, I told her a bigger and bigger lie every week. No matter what I said, the woman gobbled up my stories like candy. Mabel H. is the perfect example of the psychic's most frequent client—the credulous type. Take note that her age is a multiple of six.

Bertie shook her head sadly. It was all there—the phony hexes, the manipulations, and the escalating demands for money. But Mabel Howard was not the only person Sister Destina had cheated.

> The narcissist is driven by an overwhelming desire to be the center of attention. It is the second most common personality type I encountered as a psychic. Neglected by her husband, Penny S. paid me thousands of dollars for phony hexes and fake potions. This is, I believe, related to the number of sixes in her birth date. The number six is evil and should be eliminated entirely from modern speech.

Part diary, part academic tome, and part manifesto, the psychic's "thesis" veered wildly from subject to subject in no particular order. Topics of discussion included the Arabic numbering system, the use of the number six in Greek mythology, and the need for more electric cars.

After ten more rambling pages, Bertie put the manuscript down and rubbed her eyes. Sister Destina had mailed her thesis only hours before being brutally murdered. Why had the psychic sent her this document? Had Destina had some kind of premonition? A chill ran up Bertie's spine. The whole thing was just too creepy. Suddenly, Bertie felt a strong desire to talk to someone, anyone.

As long as they were practical, sensible, and sane.

When she heard Ellen's voice at the other end of the line, Bertie's words tumbled out in a rush of excitement.

"Girl, you will never guess what I'm reading."

"Please tell me it's not *Fifty Shades of Grey*, Bertie."

"Be serious," Bertie said. "I just found out something amazing. Are you sitting down?"

When Ellen assured Bertie that she was indeed seated, Bertie continued. "Sister Destina was a student at the U of C. The fortune-telling set-up was part of her Ph.D. research."

Ellen laughed. "I always knew those U of C folks were crazy. I just didn't know exactly *how* crazy."

"Destina mailed me her thesis the same day she was murdered. I'm in the middle of reading it right now."

"Say what?"

"You heard me," Bertie said. "Her main theory was that only certain types of people visit psychics. So far she's mentioned two: the 'credulous type' and the 'narcissistic type.' Wait a sec. Let me find the place." Delighted to have someone with whom to share her news, Bertie shuffled through the pages until she found what she was looking for. "Okay, here it is. Check this out:

"'A credulous personality, such as Mabel H., is motivated by an infantile need to live in a fairy-tale universe.'"

"I hate to admit it, but Destina's got a point there," Ellen said. "Mabel is definitely the credulous type. Did Destina write about anyone else we know?"

"Penny Swift," Bertie said. She cleared her throat and began to read.

"'Penny S. is a classic narcissist. Unused to being in an all-black environment, the woman was initially suspicious. But I soon had her eating out of my hand.'"

"Sister Destina was some manipulator," Ellen said. "It's no wonder she got herself killed. What else did you find out?"

"I'm only on page fifty. Already, I've waded through a five-page rant about the IRS, an itemized list of the shoes in her closet, and a section about her favorite TV shows. Destina hated the Discovery Channel. Can you believe it?"

"Worried someone would 'discover' the truth about her sorry behind," Ellen said. "Woman was nuttier than Aunt Harriet's fruitcake."

"I should call Mac and tell him about this thing, right?"

"Absolutely," Ellen said. "And be sure to keep me in the loop. I'm dying to know what happens next."

Later that afternoon, Bertie called Mac's cell phone.

"I discovered what may be an important clue," she said. "Do you have time to take a look at it?"

"I'm at the police station with Detective Kulicki," Mac said. "I'll swing by for a few minutes on my way home."

Chapter Sixteen

SATURDAY, OCTOBER 21—6:55 PM

It was close to seven by the time David Mackenzie appeared at Bertie's doorstep, a briefcase in one hand and a bag of Chinese take-out in the other.

"Shrimp lo mein," Mac said. "I haven't had a minute to eat all day. Be honored if you'd join me." Though his suit was wrinkled and there were lines under his eyes, the lawyer's infectious grin lifted Bertie's spirits.

"Come in, counselor," she said, waving him upstairs to the kitchen. "You look like you could use a break."

Mac laughed. "Do I really look that beat up? I didn't think it showed."

As she set the food out on the kitchen table and pulled a Michelob from the refrigerator, the burly lawyer stretched out his legs with an appreciative sigh. Tired as he was, Mac exuded a jovial masculine energy that seemed to overflow her small kitchen. Bertie suddenly wished she had not dressed so casually that morning. Instead of a Metro College sweatshirt and a beat-up pair of jeans, it would have been nice to be seen in something a bit more alluring. Not that it really mattered, of course. After all, Mac was just a friend, but still . . .

Mac lifted his beer bottle and took an appreciative swallow. "The police have found a partial print belonging to Mabel on the murder

79

weapon," he said. "But there are other prints as well, so they're interviewing all Destina's regular clients. For now, Mabel is being considered a 'person of interest,' which means the police will be watching her like a hawk."

"She's not the only person they should be watching," Bertie said. "Turns out, Sister Destina's psychic reading business was really a giant psychology experiment."

Mac put down his fork and stared in amazement. "What?"

"Destina's real name was Dustin-Destina Kingsley. She was a psych major at the U of C," Bertie said with a grin. "For some crazy reason, she sent me her Ph.D. thesis. Actually, it's not really a thesis at all. It's a deranged manifesto. Destina was using her clients like lab rats, while scamming them out of big bucks at the same time."

For the next several minutes, Bertie gave Mac a summary of what she'd learned. When she was finished, he whistled softly.

"From what you've just told me, it's likely several of Destina's clients have motives. Certainly, they all knew about that sword. Detective Kulicki says Destina kept it out in the open next to her throne."

"That's right," Bertie said. "The thing was razor sharp too. Ellen and I both saw Sister Destina use it to cut open a doll in midair." She shivered. "I suppose it wouldn't take that much strength to kill someone with a thing like that."

"No, it wouldn't," Mac said. "Killing Destina would have been easy, even for someone Mabel's size."

"Has Mabel given you an alibi for the time of the murder?"

"She admits she went to Sister Destina's house at five o'clock that afternoon. She even admits that she and the psychic had an argument. But Mabel swears that, when she left Sister Destina's house an hour later, the psychic was alive and well."

Bertie nodded. "I suppose we should not rule out the possibility that Mabel's husband did it," she said. "Charley adores his wife. If he thought anyone was trying to hurt her, he might get violent. As you know, the man has a terrible temper."

"True," Mac said. "At least he's not hanging out with Tony Roselli anymore."

"He told me the same thing," Bertie said. "Assured me that his business was completely legit. He's been a changed man since he joined the Octagon Society last year."

Mac pulled a wry face. "Can't say I'm a big fan of that bunch, Bertie. The Octagons rejected me the first time I applied, you know. Said I was not an 'established professional.' But I'm guessing it had more to do with the fact that my skin was too dark."

Bertie squirmed uncomfortably in her seat. As a tan-complected woman with somewhat Caucasian features, she had not had to deal with the intra-racial color discrimination encountered by darker-skinned people.

"The Octagons were terribly color-struck back in the day," she said softly. "I'd like to think those attitudes are different now."

"I wouldn't count on it," Mac said. His laugh was uncharacteristically bitter. "Once I'd made a big enough name for myself, they begged me to join. If it wasn't for Angie, I'd have told them to take a hike. But Angie loves being an Octagon—the parties, the fundraisers, the whole social swirl."

Figures, Bertie thought wryly. In her opinion, Angelique Mackenzie was one of the most shallow, insecure social climbers on the planet. Out of respect for Mac, she kept these thoughts to herself.

For the next few minutes, the two friends chewed their noodles in thoughtful silence.

"Have you heard anything from Angelique lately?" Bertie asked.

"She came by last night to pick up her winter coat and boots. Guess that means she's not planning to be with me this winter . . . " As his sentence trailed to a stop, David Mackenzie shook his head. "I can't get over the fact she's gone, Bertie. Five years of marriage up in smoke, just like that. For the last few days, I've been asking myself if she ever loved me. Was I just fooling myself the whole time?"

"Of course not, Mac. But you know how it is. People change. I know how brutal it can be to find yourself alone all of a sudden." She smiled and patted him gently on the arm. "But it gets more bearable with time. At least, that's what everyone tells me."

"Thanks for listening, Bertie. Most people, they don't have the time or energy to listen to anyone else's problems. It really means a lot to be able to talk to you like this."

Hoping that Mac hadn't noticed the sudden flush in her cheeks, Bertie stood up, cleared away the plates, and carried them back to the sink. *Keep this professional, girlfriend. Do not make a fool of yourself.*

When she returned to the table five minutes later carrying two steaming mugs of coffee, the lawyer was deep in thought.

"From what you've told me about Destina's so-called thesis, it's pretty clear Mabel was not her only client with a motive for murder."

"Definitely not," Bertie said. "Sister Destina was ripping off most, if not all, of them. Did you know Penny Swift was also Destina's client?"

"Swift as in Marshall Swift Department Stores?"

"The very same. Sole heir to the family fortune. The woman made the forty-six mile round trip from Kenilworth in a chauffeured limo at least twice a week. Sister Destina had nothing but contempt for her. If Penny Swift had known the psychic's true feelings, she would probably have been quite angry."

"Angry enough to commit murder?"

"I don't know the woman well enough to say, but it seems possible."

"I guess I'd better talk to her," Mac said. He sighed and rubbed a hand over the stubble on the top of his head. "I have another case going to trial next week, and I really don't have time to take on anything new. But if Mabel is formally charged, I'm going to need to get statements from everyone in Sister Destina's inner circle."

"Let me help you on this one," Bertie said, surprising herself. "Penny Swift and I know each other, at least a little bit. We had a long conversation in Sister Destina's waiting room. I think I could get her to talk to me."

Mac frowned. "You sure? What if the woman turns out to be the killer?"

"I'll be careful," Bertie said. "And very tactful. I'll have Penny eating out of the palm of my hand by the end of the interview. Anyway, you're shorthanded, Mac. You told me so yourself not five minutes ago."

The lawyer grinned and held up his hands in mock surrender. "Okay, Bertie. You win. Go ahead and talk to her. But remember, easy does it. We don't want to ruffle anyone's feathers here. I'd hate to see anything happen to you."

As she walked Mac to his car, it occurred to Bertie that she was beginning to enjoy her new role as an amateur detective. Although Mac was a brilliant lawyer, interviewing Penny Swift was going to require more of the feminine touch. The woman ran a chain of clothing stores, after all. What could be more innocent than calling her up for a bit of fashion advice?

Chapter Seventeen

The drive to Penny Swift's Kenilworth home took longer than Bertie had anticipated. For a solid hour, she drove north on Lake Shore Drive, watching the banks of heavy storm clouds rolling in over the lake. By the time she reached the Sheridan Road exit, raindrops had begun to spatter her windshield. After an additional thirty minutes spent crawling along a narrow, winding road in the pouring rain, Bertie spotted the stone pillars flanking the entrance to the Swift estate.

She turned into the driveway and drove uphill past a large tennis court. As she approached Penny's sprawling brick mansion, Bertie noted wryly that a black cast-iron coachman in a red uniform kept watch at either end of its large circular driveway. In spite of the devotion Penny Swift professed for Sister Destina, the woman apparently had no problem displaying these thinly disguised reminders of black servitude.

A white Mercedes sedan and a snazzy red Maserati were parked in the middle of the driveway. Noting with relief that the rain had stopped, Bertie parked in front of the house, being careful to leave plenty of space between her Honda and the two luxury cars. As she switched off her engine, the mansion's front door swung open to reveal a tall man in a Lacoste T-shirt, pressed khakis, and a pair of Italian loafers. His gray hair was coiffed in an elegant pompadour that matched the expensive sweater draped casually around his shoulders.

"Jesus Christ, Penny," the man shouted over his shoulder as he strode toward the driveway. "This *is* business. Can I help it if there's an emergency at the office?"

When the man had gotten about thirty feet from the house, he pulled a phone out of his pocket and punched in a number. Though Bertie could not hear exactly what he whispered into the phone, she did note that he appeared to blow a kiss into the device before sticking it back in his pocket with a satisfied smile. Clearly, everything was not all hearts and roses in the Swift household.

Choosing discretion as the better part of valor, Bertie remained inside her car while the man strode past her, angled into his Maserati, and roared away.

When she was sure the man was gone, Bertie climbed out of her car and stretched. After the rain, the temperature had dropped sharply. If she'd known it was going to be this much colder up here, she would definitely have worn a heavier coat. But at that moment, Bertie had more important things to worry about. She took a deep breath, pasted a smile on her face, and walked briskly up the flagstone walk toward the Swift mansion.

In his haste to hop into his Maserati and drive away, the man Bertie assumed to be Penny Swift's husband had left the door to their imposing mansion wide open. Bertie knocked tentatively on the doorframe and peered inside.

"It's Bertie Bigelow, Mrs. Swift. We spoke on the phone last night."

"Of course I remember you, Mrs. Bigelow. Come in," Penny said.

As Bertie's eyes adjusted to the gloom, she realized that she was standing in the middle of an elaborate Parisian-style foyer. The floor under her feet was pink marble, and an ornate chandelier hung suspended from the vaulted ceiling above her head. Directly in front of her was an elegant curved staircase. All in all, the scene reminded Bertie of something from a movie set. Perhaps in a moment Fred Astaire and Ginger Rogers would glide down those stairs and begin to waltz around the room.

But instead of Fred and Ginger, Penny Swift walked slowly down the stairs and extended her hand. Though she was in great shape and wearing an Ellesse tennis outfit that must have set her back nearly two hundred dollars, Penny Swift had a hangdog air. It didn't help that tears glistened against her tanned cheeks.

"Is this a bad time?" Bertie said. "I can come back later if you want."

"With the dirtbag I've got for a husband, it's always a bad time," Penny said, wiping her face with the back of her hand. "Come on in. I could use the company."

As Bertie walked into the living room, she noticed a wall lined with photographs of Penny and her husband from a presumably happier time: gazing soulfully into each other's eyes overlooking the Grand Canyon; in formal attire with their arms around each other at a Chamber of Commerce dinner; frolicking on their front lawn with a pudgy boy and a shaggy golden retriever.

The picture that most interested Bertie, however, showed Penny Swift dressed in white martial arts clothing. Gazing fiercely into the camera, she held a trophy in one hand and a long sword in the other.

"I see you're into karate," Bertie said. "Is that a black belt you're wearing?"

"Sixth degree Taekwondo," Penny said proudly. "Are you a practitioner?"

"Oh no. I always wanted to, but somehow, with one thing and another, I never got around to it." Bertie made a quick mental note to move Penny Swift up on the list of viable murder suspects. *For a sixth degree black belt, sticking a sword into someone's belly would be child's play. If I were this woman's philandering husband, I'd be a bit more careful.*

Smiling blandly, Bertie decided to change the subject. "Your home is lovely," she said.

Penny Swift shrugged. "Daddy bought it for me twenty years ago when Morgan and I got married. I thought we'd be happy forever.

But our son Percy's away at college now. He hardly ever visits anymore. And Morgan? Well. You know what they say, don't you?" She took a seat on the edge of a curved leather couch in the center of the room, placed her hands on her knees, and leaned forward expectantly.

Puzzled, Bertie shook her head. Was this a rhetorical question, or did the woman actually expect an answer?

"A house is not a home, Mrs. Bigelow. I believe the incomparable Luther Vandross had a hit song to that effect."

Bertie nodded. "As I said before, I'd be happy to come back another time if you'd prefer."

"Don't be silly. I want to do whatever I can to help your enquiry. Sister Destina meant the world to me. Now that she's gone, I have no idea how I'm going to cope." Penny pulled a crumpled tissue from the pocket of her tennis skirt and blew her nose. "I know Destina could be moody—downright insulting. But I didn't let it bother me. It was just part of her trickster persona."

Bertie raised an eyebrow. "From what I could tell, she was extorting money from Mabel Howard. That's a bit more severe than simply tricking someone, don't you think?"

Penny waved a dismissive hand. "Destina knew what she was doing. Mabel was a credulous flake with a pea-sized brain and money to burn. She needed an extreme adjustment to balance her karma. From each according to their means, to each according to their need."

Bertie kept her expression bland, although she found Karl Marx's words highly incongruous coming from the mouth of a North Shore socialite.

"And what about you, Mrs. Swift? Did Sister Destina balance your karma as well?"

"Of course," Penny said grandly. "That is the work of the trickster—to shake you out of your comfort zone. Rattle your cage and disorient your habitual ways of doing things. Why do you think she always wore a dress?"

"I don't know," Bertie said. "But it does seem Sister Destina went out of her way to upset people."

"Of course she did," Penny said with a smug smile. "I can see you've never done any transformational work."

"You mean workshops? Encounter groups, that sort of thing? No, I haven't, at least not yet. My husband passed away suddenly eighteen months ago, and I've been thinking about going to a support group. Does that count?"

"Not really. I'm talking about expanding one's consciousness, Mrs. Bigelow. I've done EST. Firewalking. Yogic breathwork and Ecstatic Reprogramming," Penny said, ticking each one off on her fingers as she ran down the list. "Out of all of them, Sister Destina was the best. She made me furious sometimes, but deep down, I knew it was always for my own good."

"Did you know the psychic was taking advantage of you?"

Penny Swift's lips tightened in a thin, straight line. "I had intimations."

"Was that the reason you were crying when you left Sister Destina's house the day I met you?"

"Was I? To be honest, I can't remember. Brain like a sieve, you know?" Penny giggled nervously and stood up. "I'm afraid I've been remiss in my duties as a hostess. Can I offer you a cup of coffee? Some breakfast, perhaps?"

"No thanks," Bertie said. "Mind if I ask you another question?"

"Depends what it is. Why don't you ask, and then I'll decide."

"Fair enough. You spent hours in Destina's waiting room. You watched her clients come and go. You knew Jabarion Coutze, Mabel Howard, and all the other regulars. Who do you think killed her?"

Penny cocked her well-coiffed head to the side and studied Bertie thoughtfully.

"At first, I thought it was Mabel, or perhaps her husband, Charley. He claims he doesn't associate with the Mob anymore, but I'm not sure I believe him. Then again, it could have been a burglar. Sister

Destina loved to dress up, you know. She'd walk around the house in a diamond tiara. Everyone in the neighborhood knew it."

"You're saying a burglar killed Sister Destina with her own sword?"

"Why not? The stupid thing was sitting right out in the open. Maybe the burglar forgot his gun or something." She shrugged elegantly. "As you know, it's a terrible neighborhood, riddled with crime."

Much as Bertie hated to hear this wealthy white woman speak disparagingly about the 'hood, she knew that Penny Swift was right. In the last five years, successive waves of gangs and drugs had turned the South Side of Chicago into a virtual war zone.

"You should talk to Max Sweetwater," Penny continued. "He's planning to build a new highrise complex on the corner of Fifty-Ninth and Wabash. Some of the local puritans don't like him, but Max knows the South Side like the back of his hand. Between him and Jabarion Coutze, you can find out everything you'd ever want to know about the area—who's in, who's out, and where all the bodies are buried. Hold on a minute." Penny reached into her pocket and pulled out her phone. "Let me give you his private phone number."

"I didn't know Coutze and Sweetwater were working together," Bertie said as she tapped Sweetwater's contact information into her phone. "I'd have thought they ran in completely different circles."

"You know how it is here in Chicago. Strange bedfellows and all that. Jabarion told me he was helping Sweetwater with his highrise project."

"Did Jabarion tell you anything specific about his job?"

"No," Penny said breezily. "I don't know, and I don't want to know."

"What about Commissioner Jefferson?" Bertie said. "Ever run into him at Destina's house?"

Penny Swift frowned. "Leroy Jefferson is one of those puritans I told you about—stuck in the past and afraid of change. The man's a pompous idiot. Always running off at the mouth about having been to Thailand, blah, blah, blah. I never saw him at Sister Destina's though. Was he a client?"

Now it was Bertie's turn to shrug. "I have no idea. I was just curious."

"I wouldn't get too curious about those kinds of things if I were you, Mrs. Bigelow. Those of us who saw Sister Destina on a regular basis tend to value our privacy, if you get my drift. I'd hate to see you get hurt."

On the long drive back to the South Side, Bertie mulled over what she had learned. Penny Swift had been surprisingly knowledgeable about Sweetwater's development business. Had she invested money in his Wabash Towers highrise project? She'd also intimated that she and Jabarion Coutze were friends. It seemed an unlikely alliance. Were they really that close? As she turned off Lake Shore Drive onto Fifty-Seventy Street, Bertie remained deep in thought. Penny Swift had advised Bertie not to get too 'curious' about Sister Destina's clients. "I'd hate to see you get hurt," she'd said. Had the heiress been threatening her?

That night, Bertie typed up a long report and emailed it to David Mackenzie. She should probably also have called Charley Howard to share what she'd learned in person, but she was just too tired. Instead, she fixed herself a large bowl of popcorn, poured herself a medicinal shot of brandy, and watched back-to-back episodes of *The Haves and the Have Nots* before falling into a deep and dreamless sleep.

Chapter Eighteen

MONDAY, OCTOBER 23—11:30 AM

Bertie was surprised to find herself in an excellent mood the next morning. Given the grim events of the past week, there was no logical explanation for her good spirits. Perhaps she was simply tired of being immersed in tragedy. As she walked across the parking lot toward the main entrance of the college, the crisp fall air invigorated her. The lighthearted banter of the students she passed in the hallway made her smile. She even got a kick out of the perennial bickering taking place in the faculty lounge.

While sipping her morning cup of coffee, Bertie caught the tail end of a skirmish between Ellen Simpson and her arch-nemesis, George Frayley.

"As an educational institution, Metro College should propagate an appreciation for the fine arts, Professor Simpson." The word arts came out sounding like "ahts" in Frayley's reedy New England tenor. "This so-called slam poetry festival you propose is simply not appropriate."

"What exactly do you mean by appropriate, George?" Ellen's copper bracelets jangled emphatically as she made air quotes around the word *appropriate*. "In my opinion, 'appropriate' is just another code word for poetry written by dead white men."

Looking something like a wounded polar bear, Frayley shook his head in disgust. "Be serious," he sniffed. "I am not a bigot. The

North Shore Junior League has offered to send us some volunteers. Surely, you must agree, this is a wonderful opportunity to expose the students to some real culture."

"Has it ever occurred to you that ninety percent of our students are African-American? Bringing those blue-haired ladies out here is just not going to cut it."

With a wicked grin, Ellen curtseyed and began to declaim in a pseudo-English accent:

> *I think that I shall never see*
> *A person clueless as little ole me.*
> *My old man's worth a million bucks,*
> *So who cares if my poetry sucks?*

"This is not a matter for levity, Professor Simpson," Frayley snapped. "In my thirty years at this institution, I have made it a point to teach only material of the highest quality. I will not stand by while the standards of this college are lowered in order to satisfy some benighted bureaucrat's idea of 'diversity.' Do I make myself clear?"

Ellen stuck her hand on her hip, reared back her head, and sucked her teeth ominously. "I hope you're not trying to tell me African-American poetry is inherently inferior, George. I refuse to believe that even you could be that ignorant."

With a curt nod in Frayley's direction, Ellen Simpson walked out of the room, rolling her eyes at Bertie as she swept by.

George Frayley turned to Bertie and shrugged helplessly. "What in the world is wrong with that woman?" he said. Fortunately for Bertie, this was a rhetorical question, and Frayley left without waiting for a reply.

"Wow," Amy Chu said. Coffee cup in hand, she turned to Bertie with a quizzical look. "That was *way* over the top." Metro's new computer science teacher was barely five feet tall with doll-like features and shoulder-length black hair. The large, round glasses she wore gave her a slightly owlish look. "Does this kind of thing happen often?"

"Nearly every day," Bertie said with a smile. "If too many days go by without some kind of argument, I tend to get nervous. You'll get used to it after a while."

For the rest of the day, Bertie retained her good spirits. The choir was finally beginning to get its act together. Not a minute too soon, of course. The Ace of Spades would be back in town for one final dress rehearsal before the big show on November eighteenth, which, as Bertie reminded her students on a daily basis, was less than a month away.

The only fly in the ointment was the continued absence of Melissa Jones. The chancellor had given the girl a week to apologize to Bertie and to her classmates. And after Melissa's no-show at The Ace's workshop, Terrance Witherspoon was supposed to have called Melissa's mother. But so far, Bertie had not heard a word about the girl from anyone in authority.

It was now time to rehearse "Route 66," the jaunty swing tune made famous by the great Nat King Cole. When everything went well, "Route 66" was a guaranteed showstopper. The tenors carried the melody, while the sopranos and altos chimed in with "wah, wah, wah" in harmony. But as the students began to sing, a jarring note caught Bertie's ear. She waved her hands impatiently at the accompanist, and the music stuttered to a halt.

"Altos," she said. "You are coming in late on your entrance in the third bar of letter C. I'm not sure you know how the melody goes there."

"Oh no, Mrs. B," Nyala Clark said loudly. "That ain't it. We definitely know where to come in. At least I do. The tenors are messing us up. They're not singing the music the way it's written."

The tenor section erupted in a chorus of protest. As Bertie gestured for silence, she noticed Terrance Whitherspoon sitting in the back of the room. Apparently, the dean of students had slipped in during the last few minutes. She nodded in his direction before returning to the business at hand.

"Quiet down, people," Bertie said. "It doesn't matter whose fault it is. We just need to fix the problem. Take it one more time from the top."

As the students ran through the song again, Bertie noted with relief that the problem at letter C had been corrected. At last, the group was beginning to perform as a cohesive unit. Swaying from side to side, they popped their fingers and dipped in time to the beat.

When song was over, Terrance Witherspoon applauded loudly. As the last student filed out of the classroom, he pulled out a chair next to the piano and sat down.

"Do you have a minute?" he said. "Something important's come up."

Alerted by the serious tone in Witherspoon's voice, Bertie took a seat on the piano bench across from him.

"We've got a problem," he said bluntly. "I didn't have the heart to say it in front of the students. Fania Jones is threatening to file an injunction against us."

"An injunction?" Like a boxer stunned by an unexpected blow, Bertie shook her head. "I don't understand."

"Unless Melissa is allowed to participate in the show, she's threatening to ask for an injunction to keep us from holding the concert."

"Can a judge really do that?"

"I don't know," Witherspoon said. "It seems pretty farfetched to me. Chancellor Grant and I are meeting with our lawyers this afternoon to plan a strategy, just in case she actually follows through with her threat."

"If this show is called off, there are going to be a lot of disappointed students on our hands," Bertie said grimly. "Not to mention their parents and the rest of the community. People have been looking forward to this thing for months. Do you think I should just give in—let Melissa come back?"

"Not without a written apology," Dr. Witherspoon said firmly. "This is no longer just about your choir, Bertie. It's a matter of principle. This college will not be bullied."

Bertie sighed. It was one thing to have to deal with recalcitrant students. Out-of-tune notes, sloppy rhythms—that was her domain. But an injunction was another matter entirely. If her late husband Delroy, the "African-American Perry Mason," had been there, he would have known exactly what to do. But Delroy was not there and would never be there again.

"So where do things stand now?" she said.

"At the moment, just carry on and hope for the best," Witherspoon said. "I think Fania Jones is just bluffing, trying to intimidate us. I'm still optimistic this thing will be resolved soon."

"What about The Ace?" Bertie said. "We have a contract. If we cancel this show, he's going to be furious."

"Let's pray it doesn't come to that, Bertie." Witherspoon leaned forward and flashed an infectious grin. "Is it all right if I call you Bertie? When I worked at Minneapolis College, everyone was on a first name basis. Makes for a much more relaxed and collegial atmosphere in my opinion."

"Don't tell that to the chancellor," Bertie said with a smile. "He's from the Deep South and a stickler for protocol. He sees the proper use of manners as the last bastion of civilization."

"Of course," Witherspoon said. "But when the chancellor's not around, you can call me Terry." He leaned back in his chair and winked. "Who knows, maybe Fania Jones will make us all famous. Metro College could go down in legal history as a defendant in the first ever 'right to sext' lawsuit."

"That's not funny," Bertie said, smiling in spite of herself.

"True," Witherspoon said, stretching out his legs and crossing his arms behind his head. "But at the moment, laughter is probably the best medicine. Along with music, of course. After work tonight, I intend to go home, pour myself a stiff drink, and put some Miles Davis on the stereo. Do you like jazz, Bertie?"

"You bet. No music is more satisfying to the soul."

"You got that right," Terry said. "Problem is, I'm new in town. I know about the Jazz Showcase. But I'm guessing there are even better spots tucked away in the 'hood, if you know where to look."

Bertie grinned. Metro's new dean was not only smart, capable, and good-looking—he was a jazz fan. *Amazing.*

"Do you know about the Velvet Lounge on Cermak? They've got live jazz three nights a week. Or what about the Jazz Institute of Chicago? They do a big jazz festival and other smaller events throughout the year."

Witherspoon's eyes sparkled. "Would you be willing to do me a favor? Be my tour guide to a few of the local jazz clubs?"

Is Terry Witherspoon asking me out?

As if he had read her thoughts, the dean continued hastily, "Just as friends, you understand. In the spirit of collegiality, I'll even buy the drinks."

Feeling slightly foolish, Bertie smiled. "Sounds lovely," she said.

When Bertie stopped into Rudy's Tap on her way home from work that night, she spotted Ellen Simpson sitting alone at the bar.

"Melissa Jones' mother is threatening to stop our concert," Bertie said, signaling the bartender to bring her usual glass of Merlot. "She's talking about asking the court for an injunction."

"Lord have mercy," Ellen said, shaking her head. "Nothing worse than an angry black woman. I don't know why she's condoning

Melissa's slutty behavior in the first place. In my humble opinion, the kid needs an ass whuppin'."

"She's a single mom, and Melissa is her only child," Bertie said. "I think she genuinely believes she's doing the right thing, sticking up for her daughter and all that."

"Give me a break," Ellen said impatiently. "What mother wants her kid showing her tits to strange men just so she can get a part in a show?"

"A stage mother," Bertie said simply. "You'd be surprised what people will do if they think it'll get them fame and fortune. Didn't you see the dress Kim Kardashian wore to the Grammys? Let's just say it left almost nothing to the imagination. And she's a *star*. When people like Melissa's mother see that stuff on TV, they just assume that the ability to get at least semi-naked is simply another job requirement. Her mother told me, and I quote: 'Melissa was just doing what she had to do to get noticed.'"

"Oh, she got herself *noticed*, all right," Ellen said, laughing. "But didn't you tell me The Ace actually picked her because he thought she was a good dancer?"

"That's right. Told me so himself. I was hoping he would tell Melissa the same thing. But of course, she hasn't come to class all week."

"The whole thing is a tempest in a teapot," Ellen said. "It's not going to do Melissa's career any good to cancel your show. Even Fania Jones, stupid as she is, should be able to figure that out. Speaking of stupid, I met with the Events Committee again this afternoon."

After spending the next twenty minutes discussing George Frayley's latest attempt to derail the Hip-Hop Poetry Conference, the conversation turned to Sister Destina's murder.

"Have the police arrested anyone?" Ellen asked.

Bertie shook her head. "Charley Howard has asked me to look into things. I think he's worried that Mabel might be involved. I drove out to Kenilworth to interview Penny Swift yesterday."

"That woman is a real trip," Ellen said, waving to the bartender to bring her another rum and Coke.

"You got that right," Bertie said wryly. "Turns out that the old cliché is true—money can buy a lot of things, but it does not guarantee happiness."

"Especially if you're a rich-ass white woman with race issues."

"It's more that she's got people issues," Bertie said. Every now and then, Ellen's tendency to see everything through the lens of radical politics rubbed Bertie the wrong way.

"Whatever," Ellen said with a grand wave of her hand. "Point is, Penny Swift could very well be the killer. Her relationship with Destina sounds pretty sick to me. These kinds of dependency situations have a way of turning ugly."

Bertie took another sip of her wine and nodded. "Did you know Penny was a martial arts champion? In her living room, there's a picture of her holding a samurai sword."

"Doesn't surprise me a bit," Ellen said. She turned to Bertie and winked. "Everybody knows skinny women are evil. A toothpick like Penny Swift has got enough rage inside to fillet Destina's fat ass in a heartbeat."

Bertie laughed. "Penny thinks Sister Destina was killed by a burglar. Says I should talk to Max Sweetwater—that he's an expert on the neighborhood."

"Expert, my black ass," Ellen snapped. "Exploiter is more likely. The man has evicted more black folks than Citibank." Urban renewal was another one of Ellen's pet peeves. "Younger professionals want to move back into the city, Bertie. They're tired of the boring, white-bread 'burbs where they currently reside, and they don't want to drive two hours a day in traffic just to get to work. Just a few weeks ago, a computer company bought the old Schulze Bakery on Garfield Boulevard. Pretty soon, the whole area is going to turn lily white."

Bertie sighed. "Maybe you're right, Ellen. In any case, I'm going to make an appointment to see Sweetwater. Be worth seeing what he's got to say about the murder."

Ellen shook her head. "I don't know what it is about you, Bertie Bigelow. You're such an innocent person, yet you seek out the company of scumbags."

"Guess it's my karma," Bertie said with a wicked grin.

Ellen set her drink down on the table and studied Bertie with a serious expression. "I don't think I would focus on that topic too much if I were you," she said grimly. "This is no joke, Bertie. There's a cold-blooded killer out there. If he suspects you're on to him, all the karma in the world is not going to keep you safe."

Chapter Nineteen

Tuesday, October 24—6:00 PM

As Bertie made her way down Seventy-Fifth Street, she was struck by how much the neighborhood had changed. When she was growing up, the corner of Seventy-Fifth and Paulina Avenue had been the center of a bustling commercial neighborhood. Her family had bought their meat from the small butcher shop on the corner. She'd taken her first party dress to the dry cleaners down the block and had whiled away countless hours in the Afro Pride Bookstore next door. But now, aside from a check-cashing service and a liquor store, there seemed to be little evidence of human habitation. Boarded-up store-fronts alternated with vacant lots cordoned off by spiky wrought-iron fences to prevent the neighborhood crackheads from camping there.

In this bleak environment, the offices of Max Sweetwater's company, Gilded Lily Development, Inc., stood out by a country mile. At the entrance to the parking lot, an armed guard in a crisp gray uniform emerged from his booth to take Bertie's name and license number. Only after he had located her name on his list of approved visitors was she allowed to park inside. Located in what had once been a Hi-Lo Supermart, the developer's office and its adjoining parking lot occupied the entire block. A six-foot chain-link fence topped by coils of barbed wire surrounded the complex.

As she got out of her car, Bertie was met by a clipboard-toting white girl in her mid-twenties. With her faded jeans, University of

Chicago T-shirt, and earnest expression, the girl's job could not have been more obvious if she'd had the words "Student Intern" tattooed across her forehead.

"Right this way, Mrs. Bigelow," she said. "Mr. Sweetwater's expecting you."

As Bertie followed the intern through the warren-like maze of cubicles, she couldn't help but notice that, unlike the rest of the neighborhood, Gilded Lily's office hummed with purpose and activity. Men and women of all shapes, colors, and sizes hunched over their computer terminals or whispered into headsets attached to their ears. Mounted on a wall in the center of a nest of cubicles was a huge map of the neighborhood stuck through with colored pins. Next to the map, an architect's model of a twenty-story building stood on a low wooden table.

Bertie stopped and pointed to the model. "Is this what I think it is?"

"Oh yes," the intern said proudly. "Wabash Towers. Gilded Lily's next project. It will have nineteen floors of luxury residences, with a Gap and a Starbucks at street level." She pointed to an elaborate Styrofoam parking structure filled with colored Styrofoam cars next to the building. "There will be a completely secure parking area and twenty-four-hour security on the building as a whole."

All the better to exclude the locals, Bertie thought wryly. She gave the intern a bland smile. "This will certainly change the neighborhood."

"Absolutely," the intern said without a trace of irony. "That's what Mr. Sweetwater is all about—opening up the South Side and connecting it to the rest of the city. Creating new zones of opportunity for forward-looking corporations and their investors." She blushed and then added, "I get carried away sometimes. Sorry to be blabbing at you like this. If I'm not careful, Mr. Sweetwater will be wondering what's become of us."

She led Bertie past another row of desks to the back of the building where a makeshift room had been partitioned off from the surrounding area. No doubt, this had been the store manager's office back when the building had been used as a supermarket. The intern knocked discreetly on the door and, after a suitable interval, ushered Bertie into an office as utilitarian as the cheap plywood paneling on the walls. Sweetwater may have been designing and building luxury properties, but his nerve center was far plainer than Bertie expected. Boxes bulging with manila folders lay stacked in piles on the floor. Cardboard tubes stuffed with maps and blueprints leaned in haphazard piles between the boxes.

"Good evening, Mrs. Bigelow," Max Sweetwater said. He was a hefty brown-skinned man who looked like he might have played football in college. Dressed in a rumpled brown suit, the real estate mogul's collar was unbuttoned, his tie hung loosely, and his feet rested on the edge of his desk. As Bertie entered, the intern practically genuflected on her way out, closing the door softly behind her.

"Have a seat," he boomed, waving grandly to a battered folding chair positioned across from his desk. "Sorry for the mess in here. My secretary can't keep up with the filing, I'm afraid."

As she perched on the edge of the chair, Bertie smiled. "Right now, the floor in my office is covered with sheet music. I can totally relate."

"Organized chaos," Sweetwater said. "The key to creativity." He tapped his index finger to his forehead. "It's all up here, Mrs. Bigelow. It may look like a mess, but it's my mess, and believe me, my dear, I don't miss a trick."

Of that, Bertie had no doubt.

"Quite some operation you have here," she said. "Are those students from the university you've got working for you?"

Sweetwater grinned proudly. "Grad students from the sociology department. I'm giving them a world-class lesson in urban planning, up-close and personal. Chicago is changing. If it is to survive, the South Side is going to need to change right along with it." Excited, he stood up and pointed to a map taped to the wall.

"You see this area here? Right now, it's a war zone filled with gangs, drugs, poverty, and violence. But in five years? In five years, Mrs. Bigelow, the Washington Park neighborhood will be on its way up. Did you know Obama's going to build his library here? Investors who have the foresight to see beneath the surface of things stand to reap a significant reward for their courage, believe me. The U of C knows it. That's why they're sending me these kids. The mayor knows it. That's why he's pushing to green-light my Wabash Towers project."

Bertie squirmed in her chair. The fact that its narrow bottom did not comfortably accommodate her generous rear end was only part of the problem. She was also having a hard time swallowing Max Sweetwater's relentless propaganda campaign.

"What about the people who already live here, Mr. Sweetwater? They can't afford to drink five-dollar lattes or buy their clothes from the Gap. Aren't you worried they'll be priced out of their own neighborhood?"

Sweetwater's laugh reminded Bertie of the Jolly Green Giant. "Have you been talking to Leroy Jefferson down at the zoning board? He tells me the exact same thing. But listen—since the gangs moved up here, those precious neighborhood institutions everyone is screaming about have become nonexistent. Do you know how many shootings we had in Washington Park this year?"

Although Bertie did not like to admit it, the developer had a point.

"If you're living in Washington Park these days," Sweetwater continued, "you might as well be living in Baghdad. I am doing this neighborhood a favor." He pointed to a sword encased in an elaborate lacquer scabbard and mounted on the wall next to the map. "See this? It's a samurai sword—a gift from my Japanese investors. The world is coming to Washington Park, Professor Bigelow. No matter what those shortsighted knuckleheads on the commission think."

Bertie suppressed a smile. One thing was certain—the man was passionate about his work. "I know you're a busy man, so I'll get right to the point," she said. She extracted a pen and a small notebook from her purse. "I'd like to ask you a few questions about Sister Destina. Charley Howard has hired me to investigate her operation."

Sweetwater's eyes narrowed, giving Bertie the impression of a bird dog on point. "You're working for Charley Howard? How do I know you're not in the Mafia?"

"I assume that is a joke," Bertie said curtly. "Mabel Howard is a friend of mine. Now that she's got herself mixed up in a murder investigation, Charley's asked me to talk to all of Destina's regular clients."

"I get it," Sweetwater said with a grin. "The cops think Mabel did it, and Charley's trying to dig up evidence to prove she didn't. Sorry, Mrs. Bigelow. I've already spoken to the police. At this point, I've got nothing more to say."

When Sweetwater pushed himself up from his chair to signal the end of their interview, Bertie remained in her seat.

"Mabel Howard could be arrested any day now," she said. "But I believe she is innocent, and I think you do too. Anything you can remember, no matter how small, could really help her case."

After a pause, Sweetwater sighed and dropped back into his chair. "I do not admit this to many people, but Sister Destina was my lucky charm. She'd do a reading to ask the spirits if I should buy a piece of property or not."

"You trusted her? She was ripping off Mabel, you know. Predicting dire consequences unless Mabel ponied up for expensive remedies."

Max Sweetwater shrugged. "Don't know anything about that. When Sister Destina read for me, her advice was always on the money."

"Can you think of anyone else among the psychic's inner circle who might have had a reason to kill her?"

Again, the developer shrugged. "Not really. But I will say this much. I don't believe Mabel Howard is capable of that kind of violence. The woman is about as harmless as they come. But that husband of hers? He's another matter entirely." He leaned forward and looked Bertie in the eye. "You seem like a nice lady, so let me give you some free advice. I'd be very careful what you say around that man. He's got a hell of a temper. I would not want to cross him."

As Bertie gathered herself to make an appropriate response, Max Sweetwater's telephone rang.

The developer's expression darkened as he listened intently to the voice on the other end of the phone. "Leroy Jefferson did what?" he shouted. "He can't deny my permit! We're due to break ground next month." Sweetwater listened intently for a minute, then exploded. "Christ, Beverly. This idiot is going to cost me a fortune. I've already booked a contractor, for Christ's sake. I oughta smack the daylights outta that creep." He slammed down the phone and glared into space.

Bertie cleared her throat gently. "Sounds like you've run into a problem."

"Damn right, there's a problem," Sweetwater said. "Leroy Jefferson has persuaded the zoning board to block construction on my Wabash Towers project."

"Can he do that?"

"Not for long," the developer growled. "That little SOB is going to regret this day, believe me."

"Really?" Bertie said sweetly. "How are you planning to retaliate?"

Max Sweetwater gave Bertie a startled look, as though just now becoming aware of her presence in the room. "Don't be silly, Mrs. Bigelow," he said smoothly. "Commissioner Jefferson and I are old friends. I am sure we can work it out." He pushed back his chair and stood up. "Now, if you'll excuse me, I have a few phone calls I need to make."

"Just one more thing," Bertie said. "Penny Swift told me that Jabarion Coutze is one of your employees. Is that true?"

A strange expression flitted across the developer's face. Was it irritation? Anxiety? Before Bertie could fully identify it, the look had been replaced by a bland smile.

"Is that what Penny said?" Sweetwater's booming laugh felt just a bit over the top. "I wouldn't pay too much attention to anything she says, to tell you the truth. You know how people are, Mrs. Bigelow. They tend to read things into situations they don't fully understand."

"So Jabarion Coutze does not work for you?"

"I may have slipped the kid a few bucks now and then to be my eyes and ears in the neighborhood, but it was more charity than anything else," Sweetwater said. "His daddy's in jail, you know. Poor kid's got murder in his DNA. I was simply trying to steer the boy in a more legitimate direction."

No doubt about it. Max Sweetwater was hiding something.

As Bertie Bigelow said her goodbyes and wove her way through the maze of cubicles to the front door of Gilded Lily Development, Inc., she made a mental note to speak with Jabarion Coutze as soon as possible.

There was only one problem. Coutze's father was Chicago's most notorious drug lord—a latter-day Al Capone, responsible for the deaths of at least eleven rivals. Still, if Bertie was going to dig any deeper into the mystery of Destina's murder, she was going to have to speak with the boy.

When Bertie phoned David Mackenzie at home later that evening, the burly lawyer answered his phone on the second ring.

"I've been to see Max Sweetwater," she said. "I think he was lying to me about working with Jabarion Coutze."

"Funny you should mention that kid," Mac said. "I'm supposed to meet with him tomorrow. The kid lives on the North Side near Lincoln Park. Want to come along?"

"You bet, counselor," Bertie said. "There are a few questions I'd like to ask him."

As she poured herself a celebratory brandy before going to bed that night, Bertie caught a glimpse of herself in the mirror. She was grinning from ear to ear. Her relationship with Mac was strictly business, of course. But she had to admit the idea of sitting at his side while he fired incisive questions at a possible murderer excited her. To be honest, the prospect of doing just about anything with David Mackenzie excited Bertie. More than she was willing to admit.

Chapter Twenty

As David Mackenzie's BMW inched along North Fullerton Avenue, Bertie looked out the window at the profusion of sights and sounds around her. Though it was only four o'clock, the sun hung low in the sky, backlighting the trees in Lincoln Park in a wash of autumnal color. It seemed to Bertie that everyone had chosen that very minute to savor the last remaining days of Indian summer. Purposeful professionals made their way through an obstacle course of joggers, nannies wielding oversized strollers, and elderly couples taking their poodles for a stroll. After circling the block several times in search of a parking space, Bertie and Mac got lucky when a green MINI Cooper pulled out of a space two blocks from Jabarion Coutze's brownstone.

After being buzzed into an elegant foyer and clambering up two flights of stairs, Bertie and Mac arrived at Jabarion's apartment. The door was made of polished wood and adorned with a heavy brass knocker that reminded Bertie of the ones she had seen on her last trip to London. Just as she prepared to use it, Jabarion—wearing a silk do-rag, low-slung jeans, and a sleeveless white undershirt—opened the door and waved them inside.

"Sister Destina was one of the few people who cared about me," he said in a soft, high-pitched voice. "I can't believe she's gone. Please, come in."

Jabarion's apartment featured twelve-foot ceilings and a large bay window overlooking Lincoln Park. The walls in his living room were painted a soft tangerine and lined with miniature paintings of men embracing in various positions. As Bertie sat down next to Mac on the sleek leather couch facing the window, a whip-thin white man glided into the room and placed a protective hand on Jabarion's shoulder.

"This is Roddy Frazier," Jabarion said, giving the man's hand a squeeze, "my roommate."

"And lawyer," Roddy said. His tone was light, but his eyes were hard. From the gray hair showing at his temples, Bertie guessed the man was in his mid-forties. Unlike Jabarion, he was elegantly dressed in a pair of Italian loafers, Calvin Klein jeans, and a lavender cashmere sweater. "I told Jabarion that he was not legally obligated to speak with you people, but he insisted. I am here to make sure his good will is not abused."

Mac nodded. "Not to worry, Mr. Frazier. I represent Mabel Howard, one of Sister Destina's clients. I'd like to ask Mr. Coutze a few questions."

"Fire away," Jabarion said. He took a seat in the low-slung armchair across from them and lit a cigarette. "Pay no attention to Roddy. He's just an old mother hen. I've got nothing to hide."

"Very well, Mr. Coutze," Mac said. "Tell me about the nature of your relationship with Sister Destina."

"She was my friend," Jabarion said simply. "When your father is doing time for murder, people automatically make assumptions. But Sister Destina understood me. She accepted me on my own terms."

Bertie nodded sympathetically. "It must be difficult having such a famous name."

"It's hell," Jabarion said. "People automatically assume the worst about you."

Mac leaned forward and gave the boy an appraising look. "But Sister Destina was more than a friend, Mr. Coutze. She was also your employer. What kind of work did you do for her?"

"Do you like movies, Mr. Mackenzie? Perhaps I can explain it this way. Batman is the star—the main attraction, the superhero—but he can't do his thing without Robin. Count Dracula has Igor. Captain Kirk's got Mr. Spock. You get the idea."

"So you served as Destina's lieutenant, making sure her business ran smoothly?"

"Something like that. I kept the appointment book. I showed the clients in and ushered them out," Jabarion said. "It was high theater—quite camp, really. Not meant to be taken seriously."

"Several of Sister Destina's clients took it quite seriously," Mac said sharply. "They paid thousands of dollars for phony psychic treatments. And here's something you might want to take seriously. The DA is likely to have you arrested for fraud."

Jabarion laughed. "You don't scare me, Mr. Mackenzie. Sister Destina was a very private person. She did not tell me about her treatments, and I did not ask. What she did inside that inner sanctum of hers was her own business."

"You mean to say that you knew absolutely nothing about Sister Destina's business practices?" Mac said.

"Nothing whatever," Jabarion said, ignoring a cautionary look from Roddy Frazier. "I kept her appointments. Nothing more."

Bertie leaned forward and cleared her throat gently. "But Sister Destina wasn't the only person you were working for, was she, Mr. Coutze? There's a rumor going around that you and Max Sweetwater had some kind of business arrangement."

"Who in the world could have given you that idea?" Jabarion said. "Did Sweets tell you that? My, my. Well, if anyone would know, I guess it would be him. Just bear in mind, the man has a tendency to exaggerate."

"He certainly does," Bertie said mildly. "He told me to stay away from you. Said you had murder in your DNA."

"The muthafucka said *what?*" Jabarion's hand shook as he ground out his cigarette and lunged to his feet. "That crooked bastard has got some nerve. Ask Max Sweetwater about the Home Hoodoo Program, Mrs. Bigelow. Ask him!"

Moving with the nimbleness of a dancer, Roddy Frazier positioned himself between Jabarion and his guests. "It's been oh-so-lovely chatting with you folks," Frazier said, "but my client has nothing further to say. Don't even think about coming back here without a subpoena."

It was after five o'clock by the time Bertie and Mac left Jabarion's apartment. Although the traffic on Outer Drive had slowed to its customary rush hour crawl, the two were in excellent spirits.

"Well done, Bertie," Mac said. "Jabarion would never have mentioned Destina's Home Hoodoo Program if you hadn't rattled his cage like that. I'd say we made a pretty good team in there."

Bertie felt her cheeks redden. Luckily, Mac was too busy negotiating his BMW through the bumper-to-bumper traffic to notice. As a battered pickup truck cut into the lane in front of them, he muttered under his breath and slammed on the brakes.

When the traffic began to inch forward again, she said, "This Home Hoodoo Program sounds creepy. What do you think it means?"

"Search me," Mackenzie said with a shrug. "But if the program had anything to do with shutting down Charley's restaurant, it gives Mabel an even bigger motive for the murder."

"I think Jabarion knows more than he's letting on, Mac. He was at Sister Destina's house nearly every day. I'll bet he overheard lots of useful information."

"Probably," Mac said. "But there's no way Roddy Frazier is going to let us question the boy again without a court order."

The two of them contemplated the situation in silence for the next several minutes.

"Perhaps Sister Destina discussed the Home Hoodoo Program in that crazy excuse for a thesis she sent me," Bertie finally said. "I told you about it, remember?"

Mackenzie grunted. "If Mabel ends up getting arrested, I'll have to hire a paralegal to plow through the damn thing."

"I could read it for you," Bertie said. "Poor Destina was clearly off her rocker, but I feel a responsibility, somehow. She mailed me that thesis only hours before she was killed."

"You'd be doing me a big favor," Mac said. "I'm swamped with work right now. Got three other cases coming to trial in the next month."

"No problem," Bertie said with a smile. "I'd be glad to read it for you. Truth be told, I'd do just about anything to keep my mind off the blasted choir concert."

For the rest of the trip back to the South Side, Bertie told Mac about the latest developments in her professional life—Melissa's continued refusal to apologize for her behavior and her mother's threat to take the matter to court.

"She's threatened to get an injunction to stop my concert," Bertie said. "Have you ever heard of something so ridiculous?"

Mac laughed. "Welcome to my world, Bertie. It is truly amazing, the kind of foolishness people will sue each other about. Fact is, we live in a litigious society. Bad for human relations, but very good for business."

"Fania Jones really could sue?"

"Yes. But I wouldn't worry if I were you. The college has excellent legal representation. And in the unlikely event she decided to sue you directly, I would defend you myself—make the woman rue the day she ever went to law school."

Bertie smiled. How long had it been since she felt like she had someone so unequivocally on her side—a male protector with whom she could share her troubles? David Mackenzie was one of those rare men who could be tough and gentle at the same time. And now they were teammates. Mac had said so himself.

As the lawyer's BMW turned onto Fifty-Seventh Street, Bertie had to admit she wouldn't mind at all if the relationship developed into something more.

Mac pulled into her driveway and shut off the engine.

"Take care of yourself," he said gently. He leaned across the gear-shift and kissed Bertie on the cheek. "You're a very special lady."

Chapter Twenty-One

When Bertie arrived at choir practice on Friday, Terry Witherspoon was waiting in front of her classroom.

"I'm going to need a few minutes to talk to your students," he said. "There have been some important developments."

Bertie's face sagged. "Fania Jones is going ahead with her lawsuit?"

Witherspoon nodded grimly. "She's filed for a preliminary injunction in Superior Court. There's a hearing scheduled for the middle of next week. Our lawyers remain confident they can get it overturned, but to be on the safe side, Chancellor Grant has decided to put your concert on hold until the judge issues a ruling."

After the students had filed into the classroom and taken their seats, Witherspoon delivered the bad news in crisp, no-nonsense language. The choir responded to his announcement with shocked silence, but the minute Witherspoon left the room, they exploded.

"This sucks," TyJuana Barnes said loudly. "How can they do this after all the work we put in?"

"They've got no choice," Nyala Clark snapped. "They're getting sued. Just the kind of stupid stunt you'd expect from a trashy lowlife like Melissa Jones."

"Wasn't like she was kicked out the choir forever," Maurice Green said bitterly.

"All she had to do was apologize."

"But she didn't apologize, did she," Nyala said. "Didn't apologize at all. Instead, she's ruining the show for everybody. What a bitch."

"There's no need for name-calling," Bertie said. "Anyway, I can't believe the judge is going to rule in her favor. Everything will be back to normal in a couple of weeks."

As she surveyed the angry faces of her students, Bertie hoped that her optimism was justified. And then she got an idea. An idea so phenomenal she wondered how she had failed to think of it before.

"The Ace gave me his phone number when he was here a few weeks ago," she said. "Why don't I give him a call?"

Nyala's eyes widened. "His private number? That's dope, Mrs. B. Can I have it?"

"Absolutely not. I'll give The Ace a call tonight. He was supposed talk to Melissa about the sexting thing before the workshop last week, but Melissa never showed up. Perhaps he'd be willing to talk to her over the phone. Who knows? Maybe we can get this mess cleared up once and for all."

But when Bertie telephoned The Ace later that night, she discovered that his "private number" was not nearly as private as she had hoped. Like his public number, it was monitored by a flunkie—in this case, a rude one.

"The Ace can't talk now," the man said and hung up.

If there was one thing that truly irritated Bertie Bigelow, it was rudeness. She redialed the number immediately. Even if she did not get to speak to The Ace in person, she intended to leave a message letting the singer know exactly what she thought of his staff and their manners.

The Ace himself picked up the phone on the tenth ring.

"I'm in the studio," he snapped. "Who the hell is this?"

"It's Bertie Bigelow from Metro College, Mr. Willis. I'm sorry to bother you, but something important has come up."

"Metro College?" The singer's resonant baritone jumped an octave. "I got served with court papers this morning. Me—The Ace of Spades! Can you believe that shit?"

Bertie's heart sank. "Court papers?"

"That's right," the singer said belligerently. "So if that's what you're calling about, you'll have to talk to my lawyer. I am not saying another word. In fact, I never want to hear from you people again!" As Bertie gathered herself to respond, he continued. "My manager told me not to take this gig, and now I see why. All this drama over a pair of tits!"

"But what about the students?" Bertie said desperately. "Don't you care about them at all? They are going to be crushed if this concert doesn't happen."

"Shoulda thought about that before they started sexting me, Mrs. Bigelow. I've got to make my living in this business."

Bertie's eyes filled with tears as she hung up the phone. Sighing heavily, she poured herself a shot of brandy and downed it in one swallow. It burned her throat on the way down, but with any luck, the alcohol would help her forget her troubles—at least for a while.

Chapter Twenty-Two

When Bertie finally rolled out of bed the next morning at the un-heard-of hour of eleven a.m., her head was splitting. Whether this was due to the medicinal nightcap she'd taken the night before or to the recent depressing developments in her life, she could not say. She staggered into the bathroom, swallowed an Advil, and stood under the shower until her head cleared. She was just getting out of the shower when her cell phone rang.

"Thank God you're home," Mabel Howard said. "I wanted to talk to you before I left on my trip."

"What trip?" Holding the phone first in one hand and then the other, Bertie maneuvered into her bathrobe and sat on the edge of the bed.

"That, my dear, is top secret," Mabel said in a dramatic whisper. "Let's just say, I'm onto something big—something that could break this case wide open."

Uh-oh. That did not sound good. "Have you talked to Mac? He's your lawyer, after all. You should probably let him know what's going on."

"No, Bertie, and I don't want you telling him either. I need to make this trip in secret."

"Charley doesn't know you're going?"

115

Mabel's giggle reminded Bertie of a mischievous two-year-old. "Goodness, no. It would only raise his blood pressure. You know what a temper he's got. Poor man is liable to blow a gasket."

"If you're not going to tell your husband or your lawyer, you should at least tell me where you're going," Bertie said. "What if something happens to you?"

"You're so sweet to worry," Mabel said airily, "but really, all I need you to do is cover for me. If anyone asks, just tell them I've gone to Lake Geneva for a spa weekend."

"You're a suspect in a murder investigation," Bertie said. "You can't just go waltzing off without letting people know where you're going."

Mabel's tone was a mixture of hurt and indignation. "Who do you think you are, Bertie Bigelow? The Spanish Inquisition? Just forget it, okay? Forget you ever heard from me," she said and hung up.

Frustrated, angry, and more than a little bit worried, Bertie paced around her bedroom. Should she tell someone? On the one hand, Mabel Howard was a grown woman. What she chose to do with her life was her own business, wasn't it? If Bertie called either Charley or Mac against Mabel's wishes, she was likely to lose Mabel's friendship permanently. On the other hand, this was a murder investigation. Whoever had stuck that sword in Destina's stomach was still out there, just waiting for someone like Mabel Howard to make a wrong move.

After several minutes of brooding, Bertie decided on what she hoped was a reasonable compromise. She would honor Mabel's request for secrecy for the next twenty-four hours, but if she didn't hear from Mabel by the next night, she would let both Mac and Charley know.

Though Bertie felt fairly certain she was doing the right thing, she realized it would probably be a good idea to get a second opinion. Striding briskly to the end table by her bed, Bertie picked up her phone and called Ellen.

"Mabel says she's found a new clue in Destina's murder and is going off somewhere to investigate. Think I should be worried?"

Ellen laughed. "Probably not. Knowing Mabel, it could be anything. Who knows? Maybe she's found herself a new psychic."

"Very funny," Bertie said. "The last time Mabel found a new psychic, Commissioner Jefferson got food poisoning, Charley's restaurant got shut down, and Sister Destina got murdered." She sighed. "To be honest, I just don't have time for any more of Mabel's nonsense right now. Did you know Fania Jones has filed for an injunction to stop my concert? My show is in limbo until the judge makes up his mind."

"I heard," Ellen said. "That's a tough one, Bert. You okay?"

"I am at the end of my rope," Bertie said simply. "I even called The Ace to see if he could help."

"And?"

"He basically cussed me out. Then he hung up on me. Meanwhile, the students are going nuts because their show has been put on hold. Do you think I should try to get the chancellor to change his mind? I was thinking of having the students write a petition or something."

There was a long silence at the other end of the phone. When Ellen finally spoke, her response took Bertie by surprise. "A student petition will only fan the flames, Bertie. It might even get you fired. If there is one thing our boss hates, it's controversy, as you well know. I hate to say it, but it looks like you're just going to have to wait this thing out. Pray the judge throws Melissa's she-devil of a mother out on her butt, which, I must tell you, is a very strong possibility. The woman is damn near certifiable."

"I suppose you're right," Bertie said slowly. "I just feel so powerless."

"Let the lawyers handle it. The whole situation is way above your pay grade. What you need is a little distraction. Invite your lawyer friend over for a little late-night conversation." Ellen giggled wickedly. "Gotta tell you, Bertie. That's one fine-looking brotha.

Tall, dark, and handsome. I wouldn't mind if he took my deposition some night."

"Shut up," Bertie said. Fortunately, Ellen was not there in person to see her blush. "How many times do I have to tell you? The man is married."

"In name only, my dear. Name only. Rumor has it, Angelique Mackenzie has been running up to Detroit with Waymon Reid just about every weekend. Supposedly, he's her financial advisor. But it does not take a stock market wizard to surmise the man's also invested in her more physical assets, if you get my drift." Ellen giggled wickedly again. "You're a good girl, Bertie. You want to do what's right, but let me tell you something. Life is no Sunday school picnic. There are no rules, especially where love is concerned, and the woman with the strongest will is gonna win, every time."

After a small breakfast of wheat toast and coffee, Bertie retired to her music room to spend the afternoon. Outside, the sky was gray and heavy. It would be pouring buckets before long. The wind blowing in from the lake rattled against the windows and shook the last leaves from the trees on Harper Avenue. Thank God she had the piano to keep her loneliness at bay.

When the phone rang around four thirty, she almost didn't answer it. She hated for her practice sessions to be interrupted. She wasn't expecting any calls, and what's more, she'd dealt with more than her share of drama lately. Whoever was calling would just have to leave a message, she decided. On the other hand, there was always the possibility that Mabel Howard was phoning to check in. Reluctantly, Bertie pulled herself away from the piano and answered the phone.

"I hope you haven't forgotten about our date," Terry Witherspoon said. "You promised to take me around to some of the local clubs tonight, remember?"

"Oh dear," Bertie said. The conversation she'd had with Witherspoon earlier that week about jazz clubs had totally slipped her mind. Had she made a definite date to see him? As she remembered it, the conversation had never been more than hypothetical. "Were we supposed to get together tonight?"

"Why not?" Witherspoon said. "It's as good a night as any. You live on Harper, right? I'll pick you up at eight."

Terry Witherspoon's Thunderbird rumbled into her driveway at the stroke of eight p.m. By the time Bertie opened her front door, the O'Fallon sisters had already come out to investigate.

"Lovely motor your friend's got there," Colleen chirped, raising her voice to be heard over the car's engine. "Going somewhere special?"

"Idjit! Can't you see Bertie's got a gentleman caller?" Pat grabbed her younger sister by the arm and steered her back inside.

"About bloody time, if you ask me," Colleen said as she closed the door.

Extracting his lanky frame from inside the sports car, Terry Witherspoon strode around to the passenger side and opened the car door with a sweeping gesture.

"Your chariot awaits, madame," he said.

Charmed in spite of herself, Bertie smiled and climbed in, allowing Witherspoon to close the door behind her. She couldn't remember the last time she'd gone anywhere with a new male friend. Granted, this was supposed to be a platonic outing, but nonetheless, Bertie had to admit she felt a tingle of excitement at the prospect of being out and about with such a handsome man.

"Where should we go?" Witherspoon said. "I'm not much for rap, but other than that, I'm open to anything."

"One of my former students is playing at Buddy Guy's club to-night," Bertie said.

Witherspoon whistled softly. "*The* Buddy Guy? Now I know I'm in Chicago. That man has played with everyone from Muddy Waters to The Rolling Stones."

"For years, he ran the Checkerboard Lounge on the South Side. He moved his operation downtown a couple of years ago," Bertie said. "My student was lucky to get a gig there. His music sounds a bit like George Benson, with a pinch of Parliament-Funkadelics, and a teaspoon of B.B. King thrown in. Can you picture it?"

"Definitely," Witherspoon said with a grin. "A funky guitar-driven groove with bluesy elements. I can totally get with that program."

Half an hour later, Terry Witherspoon's T-Bird rolled to a stop in front of Buddy Guy's Legends Club. After handing his keys to the valet, Witherspoon took Bertie's arm and led her inside. From the club's décor, Bertie surmised that Buddy Guy was attempting to evoke the down-home spirit of his former South Side establishment. The exposed brick walls were decorated with guitars belonging to the musical legends who'd ventured into the 'hood to jam there back in the day. Keith Richards, Eric Clapton, and of course the great B.B. King. Neon signs advertising Pabst Blue Ribbon beer illuminated the bar, and the air was redolent with the pungent smell of barbequed ribs.

But Bertie doubted Guy's downtown club would remind too many people of a South Side dive. Certainly not anyone who took a look at the prices on the menu. She felt that it spoke either to Witherspoon's tact or to the size of his paycheck that he did not blink at the prospect of shelling out thirty dollars for a pair of burgers.

"Should I try the ribs?" he said. "I'm from Memphis, and I'm picky about my barbeque. I haven't found any place here that knows how to make a decent sauce."

Bertie smiled. "If I knew you'd wanted barbeque, I'd have suggested somewhere deeper into the 'hood, but the food here is decent. They fry up a good catfish."

Witherspoon laughed. "Think I'll give those ribs a try. After living in Minnesota for the past five years, I could really use a good plate of soul food." He raised his beer glass in salute. "Here's lookin' at you, kid," he said in an imitation Humphrey Bogart accent.

"You like old movies?"

Bertie's guard dropped an inch or two when he replied, "I worship them. I keep a subscription to Netflix just so I can watch the old classics. After a stressful day, I come home from work, fix myself a bowl of popcorn, and treat myself to a double feature. Since it's all on DVD, I can fast-forward through the racist bits."

"The blackface scene in *Holiday Inn?*"

"Gone," Witherspoon said. "Ditto the antics of that brainless maid in *Gone With The Wind.*" He bugged out his eyes and waved his hands in a gesture of mock confusion. "Lawd-a-mercy, Miz Scarlet! Da Yankees is comin'. Whatever is little ole me s'poze ta do now?"

"Butterfly McQueen may have been an African-American pioneer, but it's downright painful to see her in such a demeaning role," she said.

"Exactly," Witherspoon said. "Now that I have Netflix, I don't have to put up with that mess anymore. Fast-forward has improved the quality of my movie-going experience immensely."

"I'll drink to that," Bertie said, raising her brandy Alexander in mock salute.

For the next hour and a half, she and Witherspoon swayed and tapped their feet to the sounds of G-Man Gibson, a.k.a. Gary Gibson, Metro College Class of 2011. The G-Man's licks were hot, and his backup group laid down a solid groove. Halfway into the band's second set, the checkerboard-tiled dance floor in front of them began to fill with couples strutting their latest moves. When Witherspoon suggested they join the dancers, Bertie surprised herself by saying yes.

Terry Witherspoon was a very good dancer. Dressed with casual elegance in a pair of pressed khakis, a dark-blue shirt, and a tweed jacket, he moved with an easy grace that caught the attention of several women in the room. When G-Man switched to a slow blues, it felt natural to continue dancing. As Terry pulled her close, Bertie could feel his breath on her neck and the steady pressure of his hand against the small of her back. How long had it been since she'd allowed herself to get this close to a man?

Get a grip, girlfriend, she told herself. *Don't make a mountain out of a molehill. It's just dancing—a casual night out to catch some good music.*

When the band finished their last song, Witherspoon took her arm and escorted her back to their table.

"Thanks so much for bringing me here," he said. "If it wasn't for you, I would have spent the night alone."

"Me too," Bertie said. Now that G-Man had finished playing, the tables around them began to empty.

"Yes, but at least you're not sitting in a hotel room," Witherspoon said. "There is nothing in the whole world more lonely than that, believe me."

"You're staying in a hotel?"

Witherspoon nodded. "I didn't get this job until August. By the time my contract was finalized, the semester had already begun. The college agreed to put me at the Palmer House for a couple of months, until I get myself settled."

Once again, Bertie experienced the distinct sensation of being out of her customary pay grade. The thought that Metropolitan Community College, a financially strapped inner-city institution, was footing the bill for an administrator to stay at a fancy downtown hotel floored her. Clearly Terrance Witherspoon lived in an alternative magical universe, far from the mundane world she inhabited.

"They're keeping you at the Palmer House?"

"That's right," Witherspoon said. "Would you like to see my room? It's got a great view of the city."

"Oh, I couldn't possibly," Bertie said. "I'm sure you must be tired after such a long night."

"Not at all. Come on up for a nightcap, Bertie. Have a drink. Check out the view before I take you home."

By this point, Bertie had consumed three brandy Alexanders and a massive plate of fried catfish. In the midst of this unusual combination of pleasant sensations, she felt a warning light switch on in the back of her mind. Two years ago, the late Judge Theophilous Green had lured her up to his apartment with promises of friendship and platonic conversation, only to show his true (lecherous) colors once he got her alone. There was no way Bertie was going to allow herself to be put in that position again.

"No, Terry," she said firmly. "It's been a lovely evening, but I'd like to go home now."

"Of course," Witherspoon said smoothly. If he was in any way disappointed, he did not show it.

On the way back to Bertie's house, they made agreeable small-talk about the weather, the movies they'd seen, and the musical groups they listened to. To his credit, Witherspoon did not mention Fania Jones, Bertie's choir, or Metro College.

When he parked his Thunderbird in Bertie's driveway half an hour later, she had to admit she'd thoroughly enjoyed his company. In the manner of a true gentleman, Witherspoon came around to open the passenger door. He took her hand as she clambered out of her low-slung seat, and suddenly, before Bertie knew quite what had happened, she found herself in his arms.

"You're a very sexy woman, Bertie Bigelow," Witherspoon said, brushing her cheek with his lips. "I don't mind saying, I'd like to see more of you." Tilting her chin up with his hand, he kissed her gently on the mouth.

As he kissed her again, Bertie felt the long-suppressed desires deep inside her begin to stir. But just as her libido was about to pass the point of no return, Bertie's mental warning light began to blink furiously.

"Maybe we should slow down a bit," she said, stepping back to create more space between them. "I'm new to this whole dating game."

"You sure?" Witherspoon took her face between his hands and gave her a lingering kiss.

Bertie took a deep breath. "Afraid so, Terry. I'm just not ready."

In bed that night, Bertie could still taste the hot and slightly sour tang of Terry Witherspoon's lips as they'd pressed against hers. *That is one fine man,* she thought to herself.

On the other hand, there was no denying that her sixth sense had kicked in, even as her body began to surrender. Terry was definitely good company. But could he be trusted? To be honest, Bertie would have felt more comfortable kissing someone she knew well. Someone like Mac, for example. A man with character and integrity. A proven friend who genuinely cared about her. But of course, Mac was married. Witherspoon, on the other hand, was both interested and available. But was he sincere? *The man is sexy as hell, girlfriend. What else do you really need to know?*

For the next hour, Bertie's mind wheeled in circles, trying to make sense of the startling new developments in her life. Three weeks ago, she'd been a lonely widow, crying herself to sleep in an empty bed. Now here she was, kissing a man she barely knew and at the same time (if she were to be totally honest) lusting after David Mackenzie, a married man.

What she needed was a second opinion, preferably from an expert. Fortunately, Ellen was available to meet her for brunch the following morning.

Chapter Twenty-Three

When Bertie and Ellen arrived at the Mellow Yellow restaurant for brunch the following morning, the place was packed. A mixed crowd of older middle-class blacks, scruffy-looking students, and affluent professional types clustered around the small bandstand wedged against the restaurant's large plate-glass window. As they nodded their heads in approval, a skinny white girl belted out Billie Holiday tunes, accompanied on guitar by a Japanese boy with a ponytail.

Taking what was most likely the last available table in the entire restaurant, Bertie and Ellen squeezed between a brick wall and the doorway to the men's room. Not the most salubrious of locations, but the two women were so involved in their conversation, they barely noticed.

"Why didn't you tell me?" Ellen's tone was not exactly angry, but Bertie could tell her friend's feelings had been hurt. The fact that Bertie had gone on her first date in nearly a year without letting Ellen know was a serious breach of girlfriend etiquette.

"It all happened so suddenly," Bertie said, lifting her hands in apology. "I barely had time to do my hair and pick out a decent dress before it was time to go."

Ellen grunted. "If you'd just taken two seconds to call me, I could have saved you a world of trouble."

125

"What kind of trouble?"

"As we both know, I've had my share of adventures where men are concerned," Ellen said slowly. "So I hope you won't take what I am about to say the wrong way."

"Of course not," Bertie said, waving her hand in an unsuccessful attempt to get the attention of the harassed waitress clearing the table across from them.

"I am sorry to be the one to tell you, but . . . "

"But what, Ellen? For Pete's sake, stop beating around the bush."

Ellen sighed. "It guess it's better you hear it from me than from someone else." She surveyed the room closely before continuing. "My friend Raeline called from Minneapolis last week. When I mentioned Witherspoon's name, she started cussing a blue streak. Terry Witherspoon is trouble, girlfriend. He pulled the exact same seduction routine on Raeline five years ago. After he'd gotten what he wanted, he dropped her like a used Kleenex."

"Five years is a long time," Bertie said, ignoring the hurt she felt inside. "Who's to say he hasn't changed?"

"His wife, most likely. Raeline says Terry is very much married to a white woman in Minneapolis. The woman has been known to hire detectives to follow anyone she suspects of being involved with her husband. I wouldn't be surprised if she is on her way to Chicago this very minute."

Bertie's stomach roiled. She no longer cared if the waitress ever made her way back to their table.

"You sure?"

Ellen nodded grimly. "You were probably going to be Witherspoon's last fling before Wifey Dear blew into town."

Bertie stared at the wooden table in front of her, trying her best to not let Ellen see how disappointed she was.

"I should have known it was too good to be true," she said bitterly. "I feel like such a chump. How could I have been so stupid?"

Ellen patted her friend consolingly on the hand. "You didn't know, that's all," she said.

"Well, actually, I did kind of know," Bertie said slowly. "It was in Sister Destina's prediction. She said three men would pursue me, remember? An old friend, a new friend, and a false friend. I guess Terry was the false one."

"Nonsense," Ellen said, shaking her head. "If Destina was such a psychic hotshot, how come she let herself get murdered? No, Bertie. There's nothing occult about this situation. This is just the oh-so-common dilemma of being a single black woman in this predatory age."

"If you say so," Bertie said glumly.

"Let's order a massive breakfast and eat ourselves into a coma," Ellen said, waving to the waitress. "Nothing like two thousand extra calories to help a girl forget her troubles."

When her cell phone went off at midnight, Bertie was severely tempted not to answer. Whether it was Terry Witherspoon calling with another jive-time come-on or Eberhardt calling with more bad news about the lawsuit, she felt certain that answering the call would only lead to more misery.

Trapped inside her cell phone's tinny speaker, Marvin Gaye sang the refrain to "What's Goin' On" over and over. Muttering a few unprintable words under her breath, Bertie answered it against her better judgement.

"Sorry to call you so late," Mabel Howard whispered. "I wanted to let you know I'm okay."

Bertie pressed the phone closer to her ear. "Speak up, Mabel. I can barely hear you. Where are you?"

"I'm in St. Louis with Jabarion Coutze."

"You're what?"

Oblivious to the late night chill, Bertie threw off the covers and got out of bed.

"We're attending the Bishop Hayes Self-Empowerment Conference. You've heard of the bishop, right?"

Of course Bertie had heard of him. Taking his cue from pop psychology, the popular televangelist emphasized personal responsibility and the power of prayer. His central tenet, "The Lord Helps Those That Help Themselves," was emblazoned in gold letters above the doorway of his ten-thousand-seat megachurch.

"Jabarion and I are turning over a new leaf," Mabel said. In a rambling monologue, she described the highlights of the conference: the bishop's five-hundred-voice choir, his hands-on healing sessions, and his marathon sermons. "Jabarion and I were in victim consciousness. We gave our power away, let Sister Destina rule our lives," she said. "But all that's over now. We are free."

Before they ran off to St. Louis, Jabarion had given Mabel a blow-by-blow account of Sister Destina's Home Hoodoo Program.

"Sweetwater would target homeowners in areas that were near the University of Chicago that had not yet gentrified," Mabel said. "He'd have Jabarion call to see if they'd be interested in receiving a free consultation from a 'distinguished and reputable psychic.'"

"Did it work?" Bertie said. "I usually hang up when I receive calls like that."

"Yes, but that's you," Mabel said. "The people Sweetwater targeted were elderly, lonely, and vulnerable. They stay barricaded inside because the neighborhood is so dangerous. You'd be surprised how happy they are to have someone to talk to."

"Jabarion can be very smooth when he wants to be," Bertie said, remembering how he'd kissed Penny Swift's hand in Destina's waiting room.

"A lovely boy," Mabel agreed. "He's totally broken up about this thing, Bertie. His part in it, I mean. That's why he spilled the beans."

"So what would happen next?"

"Destina, dressed as a man in a suit and tie, would pay the home-owner a visit. After accurately predicting a few minor life events in order to win their trust, she would move in for the kill. In vague and somewhat mystical language, she'd tell them their home was a nesting place for toxic vibrations. Tell them she saw tongues of fire licking at their heels."

"Tongues of fire?"

"That's right. As you remember, Destina could be quite dramatic. By this point, the poor homeowner would be shaking in their rocking chair, believe me. Then she'd make the pitch. 'The spirits are with you,' she'd say. 'You will soon be given an opportunity to make a profit from your property.' Naturally, she'd recommend they contact Max Sweetwater."

"Most homeowners are not that superstitious," Bertie said. "What about the people who either didn't want to sell or wanted a lot of money for their homes?"

"Most people are greedy," Mabel said. "If they thought they were putting one over on Sweetwater by selling him a house that was about to burn down, they were happy to sell. And for those who didn't, Jabarion Coutze would set a small fire at their house a few days later. Not enough to burn the place to the ground, but enough to diminish its value significantly. One way or the other, Sweetwater acquired the property at a bargain price."

"Didn't anyone go to the police to complain?"

"Be realistic," Mabel said in a pitying tone. "This is the ghetto. Nobody goes to the police about anything if they can help it."

"Okay," Bertie said slowly. "But what does any of this have to do with the murder?"

"Sister Destina called me the day she was killed. She'd had some kind of conversion experience and was trying to put things right. Said she was sorry for all the phony hexes she'd laid on me and asked me to come by the house."

Bertie inhaled sharply. "You were at Sister Destina's house the night of the murder?"

"I know it doesn't look good, Bertie, but that's what happened."

"This is definitely not going to help your case," Bertie said.

"The police can say what they like," Mabel said airily. "I was not the last person to see Sister Destina alive, and I can prove it. Max Sweetwater drove up as I was leaving. Bet you a hundred to one he's the killer."

"If what you say about the Home Hoodoo Program is true, Max Sweetwater and Sister Destina were in business together. Why would he want to kill her?"

"Sister Destina told me she'd had some kind of apocalyptic vision of good and evil. People touched by Satan, that kind of thing. I think it scared the living daylights out of her. She was trying to clean up her act and bring her karma into balance."

"I suppose that makes some kind of sense," Bertie said slowly. "If Sister Destina was going to blow the whistle on his Home Hoodoo scam, Sweetwater would clearly have had a motive. But this is all just conjecture."

"No, it isn't," Mabel said smugly. "I have proof. Max Sweetwater keeps a logbook in his office safe of the homeowners he targeted to receive the hoodoo treatment. The book lists the owner's name, address, and the date they consulted with Sister Destina. A check mark next to the address indicates whether the house was scheduled for a fire hex."

"A book like that would be pretty damning evidence," Bertie admitted. "I suppose Mac could try to get a subpoena to search Sweetwater's office, but it doesn't seem likely the court would issue it. Jabarion Coutze is the son of a convicted felon. Why would any judge believe him?"

"Would you have a little faith, please?" Mabel said impatiently. "We don't need to worry about a subpoena. I'm going to get the book myself."

"But how do you even know Sweetwater will see you?"

Mabel giggled mischievously. "I have an appointment, of course. I told Sweetwater I wanted to sell Charley's restaurant. It's right in the heart of Bronzeville—a very up-and-coming neighborhood. Sweetwater was practically drooling by the time I got off the phone."

"And I suppose you also have a plan for how you're going to get him to show you this logbook?"

"Don't you worry," Mabel said. "I have my ways. Tell Charley and Mac to meet me at Sweetwater's office tomorrow night. You come too, Bertie. Eight p.m. I'm about to blow this whole case wide open."

Chapter Twenty-Four

MONDAY, OCTOBER 30—9:00 AM

When Bertie reached Mac on his cell phone the next morning, he was less than thrilled to learn that his client had left the state without his knowledge. And when Bertie let it slip that she'd known about Mabel's travel plans, the lawyer's displeasure deepened.

"You knew Mabel was in St. Louis and didn't tell me?"

"Not exactly," Bertie said. "She told me she was going away but wouldn't tell me where."

"You should have called me immediately," Mac said. "Mabel Howard is my client. More to the point, she is a suspect in a murder investigation. What in the blue blazes were you thinking?"

If there was one thing Bertie hated, it was being reprimanded.

"I'm calling you now, aren't I?" she replied. "The trip is water under the bridge now, anyway. The point is, Mabel's discovered some important new information."

"And rather than share this so-called important information with me, her lawyer, Mabel told you instead?"

"What was I supposed to do, Mac? As soon as I found out something useful, I called you." Although she understood Mac's frustration at being left out of the loop, Bertie felt her temper rising. She and Mac were colleagues, after all. Working together to catch a vicious killer. But in that moment, Mac's tone was decidedly less

132

than collegial. "Mabel says that Sister Destina, Max Sweetwater, and Jabarion Coutze were involved in a fraudulent real estate scam."

The lawyer snorted in disgust. "And how did Mabel come by this information? Did she read it in her horoscope? Oh, I know. She got it off the Psychic Hotline."

"This is no time for sarcasm," Bertie snapped. "The fact that your client left town without telling you is not my fault. You asked me to help you with this case, didn't you? Mabel wants us to meet her at Max Sweetwater's office tonight at eight. Don't be late."

As she hung up the phone, Bertie shook her head ruefully. Only yesterday, she'd been daydreaming about David Mackenzie. She'd even gone so far as to imagine what it would feel like if he took her in his arms. How sweet his lips would taste if he kissed her. *What a fool I've been,* Bertie thought bitterly. Mac was a smart, capable, and honest person, to be sure, but there was no way Bertie wanted to be around anyone who could speak that sharply to her. No way at all.

Her next phone conversation was even more difficult.

"My wife did what?" Charley Howard's voice was so loud she had to move the phone away from her ear. "She told me she was going to Lake Geneva. Of all the low-down, dirty, devious tricks." In the background, Bertie could hear him slamming his fist against a wooden surface. "Don't you remember why I hired you in the first place? You were supposed to be my eyes and ears, Bertie. But you lied to me instead."

"Not exactly." A feeling of déjà vu descended as Bertie explained for the second time that morning that Mabel had sworn her to secrecy, but the idea of honor between girlfriends cut no ice with Charley Howard.

"You are fired, little lady," he snapped. "And don't even think about trying to collect any money for the time you've put in so far. No siree. I do not give my money away, especially to people who stab me in the back."

"You can be mad at me all you want," Bertie said. "But give your wife the benefit of the doubt. She's found some important new evidence in the case. If she's right, this evidence will exonerate her and point directly to the guilty party. She wants us to meet her at Max Sweetwater's office tonight at eight o'clock."

For a full minute, there was silence at the other end of the phone.

"You sure this is a good idea?" Charley finally asked.

"No," Bertie said, "but what choice do we have? You don't want Mabel uncovering a murderer by herself, do you?"

"You've got a point. Maybe I better call a couple of guys I know to come along for the ride."

"I'm sure that won't be necessary," Bertie said hastily. "Mac will be there to keep things from getting out of hand."

"All right, little lady. You're on. Gilded Lily Developers on Seventy-Fifth Street. See you tonight at eight."

Bertie felt nervous and unsettled for the rest of the day. Twice during Music Theory 101 she lost her train of thought in midsentence. During choir rehearsal, she stared off into space until the sound of Nyala Clark tittering in the back row snapped her back into the present. Truth be told, Bertie and her students were all feeling aimless. There was little point in rehearsing for a concert that had been put on hold indefinitely. Did it really matter if some of her students could not tell the difference between an eighth note and a hard-boiled egg? In the end, did anybody really care?

After forty-five dispiriting minutes, Bertie dismissed the choir and retreated to the faculty lounge. The room was empty except for Ellen Simpson, who sat on the couch leafing through a pile of student essays.

"You look depressed, girlfriend," Ellen said. "Don't tell me you're still upset about that jive-ass Terry Witherspoon. That man is not worth a single tear."

"Honestly? I don't even know what I'm so depressed about," Bertie said. "Life has gotten so complicated recently. Between this lawsuit, my pathetic love life, and Sister Destina's murder, I am totally distracted. I barely got through my lecture today."

"How about stepping 'round the corner to Rudy's Tap with me? A nice soothing glass of red wine is bound to lift your spirits."

Bertie shook her head glumly. "I can't. I'm supposed to meet Mabel at Max Sweetwater's office tonight."

"What for? More detective stuff?"

"Something like that." Ellen listened eagerly while Bertie related the latest developments in the murder investigation. "Mabel claims she's going to reveal some big secret tonight. Something that may uncover the identity of the murderer."

"Girl, you've got no right to be depressed," Ellen said. "You're like the black Miss Marple or something. Would it be okay if I came along? I've never been part of a murder investigation before."

"You'll probably be disappointed," Bertie said. "The way my life's been going lately, the trip is likely to be a complete waste of time."

"In that case, we'll go have a drink after," Ellen said with a grin. "Anyway, you might need some backup."

"You're not worried things might get dangerous?"

"I'd love it." Ellen's eyes sparkled with excitement. "If you think it's going to get really hairy, we can swing by my apartment and pick up my .22. It's just a little gun, but it packs a wallop, just the same."

"Absolutely not, Ellen. We are not walking in there and waving guns around." When she saw the wounded expression on her friend's face, Bertie relented slightly. "I know you mean well, but I don't think we are going to need weapons. Mac and Charley are going to be there to help us out. I'm sure we can handle anything that comes up."

"Did you say 'we'?" Ellen said with a grin. "All right, partner! Let's hustle our butts out there."

"It's too early," Bertie said. "The meeting doesn't start till eight. It's only six thirty."

"Get a grip, Bertie. I thought you were a *detective*. Don't you know the detective always goes to these kinds of meetings early? You need to case the joint—get the lay of the land and all that stuff."

"I know the lay of the land," Bertie said. "I've been there before."

"Not with me you haven't. I'll even do the driving. Let's get a move on, shall we?"

Thirty minutes later, Ellen pulled her car in front of Gilded Lily Development, Inc. This time, the gate to the parking lot was up, and the guard who had admitted Bertie on her last visit was nowhere to be seen. With a shrug, Ellen pulled her vintage Volvo station wagon past the empty guard station and into the lot. The other two cars in the lot were parked close to the side entrance of the building. One of them was a maroon Cadillac Escalade tricked out with whitewall tires, tinted windows, and a matching sunroof.

"That's got to be Sweetwater's ride," Ellen said, pulling into the adjacent space. "No doubt purchased with the money he's made throwing hard-working families out of their homes."

"Ellen, please," Bertie said sharply. "If you don't think you can be calm, maybe you should wait in the car."

"Don't worry," Ellen said. "I was only kidding. When we get inside, I'll be silent as a mouse." Ellen tilted her head in the direction of Sweetwater's car. "Just between you, me, and the gatepost, though, Bertie, tell the truth. Isn't that exactly the kind of pretentious heap you'd expect a guy like Max Sweetwater to drive?"

To change the subject, Bertie said, "Looks like Mabel is here as well." She pointed to the cherry-red Jeep with a vanity plate that read MAGIC GRL.

"If that's the case, what are we waiting for?"

Forgetting all about her promise to stay quiet and remain in the background, Ellen jumped out of the car and strode briskly toward the building. Not wanting to be left completely in the dust, Bertie trailed along behind her. It would probably have been prudent to wait for Charley and Mac to join them, but it was too late now.

"Look, Bertie. Someone left the side door propped open. They must be expecting us."

A brick had been wedged into the side doorway where the eager young intern had met Bertie on her previous visit. Hoping that her friend's supposition was correct, Bertie followed Ellen into the apparently deserted office building. The large florescent lights that had lit the place during Bertie's first visit had been turned off. The eerie glow of the office's many computer screens provided the only illumination. Fortunately, Bertie had been there before. Surprised at the accuracy of her memory, she led Ellen through the maze of cubicles toward Sweetwater's office. When they passed the Styrofoam model of Wabash Towers, Ellen whistled softly. The model, illuminated by a small floodlight, looked remarkably lifelike.

"So this is what the bastard's been up to," she said, pointing to the Styrofoam name plates listing the Tower's proposed tenants. "Starbucks. J. Crew. The Gap. Not a single black-owned business, Bertie. Sweetwater is selling our neighborhood out to The Man."

"He's selling our neighborhood to the people who will make him the most money," Bertie said tartly. "But it doesn't matter now. In a couple of minutes, you can talk to him in person. His office is just around the corner."

Grabbing Ellen by the hand, Bertie turned toward the narrow passage that led to Sweetwater's office. As the two women left the circle of light illuminating the model of Wabash Towers, they were once again plunged into total darkness.

Suddenly, they heard a high-pitched scream. Chilled to the bone, Bertie and Ellen ran toward the source of the sound. As they rounded the final corner, they found Max Sweetwater's office door wide open. All the lights were on in the room. Framed against the light, Mabel Howard stood, sobbing uncontrollably. At her feet lay Max Sweetwater. The developer's rumpled brown suit, his desk, the walls, and every other surface in the room was covered in blood.

"Oh my God!" Bertie shrieked. "Oh my God! Mabel, what happened?"

Mabel Howard did not answer. Sweetwater's Japanese sword dangled limply from the fingers of her right hand. Like her dress and her overcoat, the weapon was stained with blood.

Showing surprising calm for someone who'd just come along for the ride, Ellen Simpson pulled out her cell phone and dialed 911. Seconds later, Mac and Charley ran into the room. As Mabel continued to stand motionless over Max Sweetwater's body, Charley gently removed the sword from her hand and laid it on the floor.

"Mabel, honey, look at me," he said. "What happened here?"

"It would be best if Mabel kept quiet," Mac said taking a quick look around the room. "Don't anybody touch anything. Have the police been notified?"

"They're on their way," Ellen said. "I just called them."

Mac grunted. "Which means you people have just ten minutes to tell me what happened here. Starting with you, Bertie."

"As you know, Mabel asked me to meet her here," Bertie said quickly. "Ellen volunteered to come along. When we walked in, Mabel was standing over the body. Honest, Mac. That's all I know."

As Bertie spoke, Mabel continued to stand with a blank expression on her face. Charley wrapped a protective arm around her shoulders and led her away from Sweetwater's corpse.

"This man's throat has been cut," he said, shooting Bertie an angry glare. "This is all your fault, Bertie. You were supposed to be keeping an eye on her."

"Are you saying this murder is my fault?" Bertie replied angrily. "God knows, I've been doing the best I can to keep Mabel out of trouble. That's why I came here in the first place."

"Quiet, both of you," Mac said curtly. Waving Charley to step aside, he touched Mabel gently on the arm. "Mabel, I'm your lawyer. Whatever happened here, you've got to tell me. I promise I will do my very best to keep you out of jail, but I can't do that if you won't talk to me. Understand?"

Mabel Howard blinked and gave Mac the tiniest of nods.

"Good," the lawyer said. Speaking very slowly, as if talking to a small child, he continued. "The police will be here very soon. Before they come, I need you to tell me if you did this. Did you use that sword to kill Max Sweetwater?"

Just as Mabel was about to respond, Detective Michael Kulicki and three uniformed policemen burst into the room.

Chapter Twenty-Five

TUESDAY, OCTOBER 31—4:00 PM

When Bertie arrived at Rudy's Tap the following afternoon, the place was deserted. She'd had a long, hard day at work and was in desperate need of liquid refreshment. She took a seat at the bar and ordered a glass of Merlot. As Bertie nodded her head appreciatively in time to The Jazz Crusaders cut spinning on the jukebox, Ellen slid onto the next barstool.

"The police give you a hard time last night?" Ellen caught the bartender's attention and ordered a rum and Coke. "Tell me everything."

"Detective Kulicki had trouble believing that I just stumbled upon the corpse by accident."

"Why on earth would the man have a problem with that?" Ellen said with a wry grin. "This is only your second dead body this month. It's not like you do this every day."

"Ha ha, very funny," Bertie said. "Somehow the detective failed to see the humor. He kept asking the same questions over and over. I don't think he believed a word I said. It was after midnight before I got home."

"He was tough on me too, at least until he realized I didn't have a clue."

"Charley Howard fired me last night," Bertie said. "Told me I was the worst detective he'd ever seen."

"Good," Ellen said. As Bertie opened her mouth to protest, Ellen raised a cautionary hand. "You did the best you could, Bertie. Was it your fault Mabel got herself hooked on that crazy psychic? Of course not! The whole situation was messed up long before you got in the picture."

For the next few moments, the two women sipped their drinks in silence.

"If I were Charley, I'd be asking myself what Mabel was doing with that sword in her hand in the first place," Ellen said.

Bertie sighed. "I know it looks bad, but I still can't believe she's a killer."

"What does Mac say? Have you talked to him yet?"

Bertie shook her head. "After the cops came in, they put us in separate rooms. I haven't seen or heard from him since. I think he's still mad that I didn't tell him about Mabel going out of town."

"That's a man for you. Always looking for someone to blame when things go wrong." Ellen put down her glass and winked broadly. "I wouldn't let it bother you, though. He'll calm down in a bit. I'm telling you, girlfriend, Mac's got the hots for you. I've got radar. I can sense these things."

All the way home from Rudy's Tap, Bertie brooded. Could it be that Ellen was right about Mac's interest in her? If so, why did this possibility leave her feeling so unsettled? Bertie had always prided herself on being a clear-thinking and decisive person. It was not at all like her to develop crushes on men, particularly men with whom she was involved professionally. And yet, here she was, kissing Terry Witherspoon one minute and daydreaming about Mac the next. Whatever craziness was bubbling up in her hormones, it was time to bring her feelings under control.

For the rest of the way home, Bertie hummed songs by strong, self-reliant women: "Superwoman" by Alicia Keys; "I'm Every Woman" by Chaka Khan; and finally a rousing chorus of R-E-S-P-E-C-T, complete with a few Aretha-like flourishes.

Bertie had almost begun to feel like her old self again by the time she pulled to the curb. As she got out of the car, a trio of young girls in princess costumes scurried excitedly across the street.

"Good grief," Bertie said to no one in particular. She'd been so preoccupied with the craziness going on in her life, she'd forgotten all about Halloween.

Next door, the O'Fallon sisters had a large inflatable pumpkin set up in their driveway to celebrate the occasion. Dressed as Batman and Robin, the two women stood on their front porch, passing out candy to a stream of costumed children.

"Oh my goodness" Colleen cooed. "It's Freddy Krueger from *Nightmare on Elm Street!*"

"Ya scared me witless, young man," Pat said, dropping a fist full of Hershey's Kisses into the child's outstretched shopping bag. "Truly, ya did."

If this had been a normal Halloween, Bertie would have joined them, but at the moment, the idea of celebrating anything even remotely macabre was more than she could handle. Instead, she gave the two elderly sisters a friendly wave and scurried inside. After turning off her porch light and fixing herself a Lean Cuisine dinner, she immersed herself in a deliciously frothy Terry McMillan novel. At ten p.m., she crawled under the covers and turned out the light.

But the minute she closed her eyes, a host of disturbing images began to flash through her mind: the vacant expression on Mabel's face as she stood over Sweetwater's body; Jabarion Coutze simpering as he escorted Penny Swift into the inner sanctum; Sister Destina splayed across her throne, her elaborate white wedding dress covered in blood.

After tossing and turning for another forty-five minutes, Bertie got out of bed, pulled on her bathrobe, and padded downstairs to the kitchen to fix a cup of tea.

Technically speaking, of course, Mabel's guilt or innocence was no longer Bertie's concern. Charley Howard had fired her. The most logical thing for her to do was to stop worrying about the case. But deep in her heart, Bertie knew that this was not possible. Mabel was her friend. If Bertie ever wanted to sleep at night again, she was going to have to figure this thing out. Whether Charley Howard liked it or not.

It had been ten days since she'd looked at Sister Destina's so-called thesis. Though the manuscript was rambling and chaotic, it was still possible it might contain a valuable clue. Bertie carried her cup of double-strength Irish Breakfast tea upstairs to her work table and lifted Destina's manuscript from its cardboard box.

> The dependent type is a common visitor to any psy-chic's office. Jabarion C. is weak, both emotionally and physically, but there is hope that, under my expert tutelage, he will someday become a man. To sharpen his inner warrior, I have entrusted him with my Home Hoodoo Program. The program was suggested to me by Max S., a perfect specimen of the predator type. The predator is the lion of the psychic jungle.

Bertie grinned. At last, she had found independent proof of Mabel's allegations.

But for the next twenty pages, Destina rambled on about the feeding habits of lions in the jungle with no further mention of either Sweetwater or the Home Hoodoo Program.

It was now nearly two o'clock in the morning. Exhausted, Bertie put the manuscript back in its box and climbed into bed.

Chapter Twenty-Six

As Bertie took her seat next to Terry Witherspoon in Chancellor Grant's office the following morning, she could barely contain her anxiety. Under normal circumstances, she would have enjoyed the panoramic view of the campus afforded by the chancellor's large picture window. She might even have appreciated the polished sheen of his mahogany desk and the plush shag carpet under her feet.

But these were not normal circumstances. Not at all.

"Mrs. Jones' request for a preliminary injunction has been denied," Chancellor Grant announced in his ponderous baritone. "However, she has informed our lawyers that she intends to appeal the ruling."

Bertie took a deep breath and stole a quick glance at Terry Witherspoon, who looked straight ahead with an impassive expression.

"The appellate court will hear her argument at the end of the week," the chancellor continued. "Meanwhile, the larger question of whether we have violated Melissa's constitutional right to free speech remains unresolved. Mrs. Jones is also suing the college on that matter. She is asking for the sum of one hundred million dollars in punitive damages. A trial date on that issue has been set for December fifteenth."

Bertie cleared her throat. "Is there any way Melissa's mother could be persuaded to reconsider?"

"Dr. Witherspoon tried that route, Professor Bigelow. He spoke to Mrs. Jones on the telephone last week. Unfortunately, she refuses to change her mind."

"Yes, but what if I spoke to her," Bertie said. "Melissa is a natural-born performer. I can't believe she wants this show to be cancelled any more than we do. Surely I can persuade Mrs. Jones that denying her daughter the opportunity to participate in this show is not in anyone's best interest."

"Unfortunately, it is now too late for further negotiation," Chancellor Grant said. "Our lawyers have indicated it would be unwise to contact the girl as long as the case remains active."

"So where does that leave us?" Bertie said. Though she was trying to maintain a professional demeanor, her words tumbled out in a jumble of anxiety. "The Ace, I mean Mr. Willis, was giving this performance free of charge, as a service to the community. He's let me know, in no uncertain terms, that if this concert is cancelled, he will not reschedule. To be honest, he was quite angry about the whole thing."

The chancellor grunted. "I shouldn't wonder. Any thoughts, Dr. Witherspoon?"

Again, Bertie shot a quick glance in Witherspoon's direction, but the dean's expression was unreadable.

"Professor Bigelow allowed Melissa to get out of control," Witherspoon said crisply. "If she had exercised a firmer hand in the classroom, this entire incident could have been avoided. At this point, however, the only reasonable alternative is to cancel the concert and move on."

Bertie could hardly believe her ears. Was Witherspoon trying to blame her for the sexting fiasco?

"I take strong exception to Dr. Witherspoon's remarks," Bertie said. As Witherspoon flicked an imaginary piece of lint from his pant leg, she felt like screaming. Instead, she took a deep breath and continued in a crisp, professional tone. "If I had known that Melissa was going to send naked pictures of herself to our visiting artist, I would certainly have stopped her. As soon as I found out, I reported the matter to Dr. Witherspoon, who assured me he had prior experience with this sort of thing. He was the one responsible for talking to the girl's mother, not me. If anyone is to blame, I suggest you look in his direction."

As Witherspoon opened his mouth to respond, the chancellor cut him off.

"Let us not bicker, please. I understand that this is an upsetting situation, but to argue about whether it could have been prevented or not is pointless at the moment. The question before us at present is whether we should try to push forward with this concert or not." Chancellor Grant leaned his considerable bulk backward in his chair and gazed up at the ceiling, as if seeking inspiration. "Mrs. Jones has told our lawyers that she will pursue this matter all the way to the Supreme Court if necessary. Personally, I suspect the woman may be somewhat unhinged. However, given the circumstances, I must agree with Dr. Witherspoon." Ignoring the stricken look on Bertie's face, Chancellor Grant pushed back from his desk and stood. "The Metro College Choir concert is now officially cancelled. I will instruct our legal team to telephone Mr. Willis and inform him of my decision."

Too stunned to speak, Bertie willed herself out of her chair, nodded brusquely in Chancellor Grant's direction, and left the room. She kept her game face on as she swept past Hedda Eberhardt's desk, strode down the hall, and rode the elevator down to the basement. Only after she had entered the ladies' room and locked herself safely in a stall did Bertie Bigelow burst into tears.

I actually thought Terry Witherspoon wanted to be my friend, she thought bitterly. Instead, the man had done his level best to stab her in the back. Bertie did not believe for a single moment that Witherspoon actually thought she could have prevented the sexting incident. He'd simply been trying to make her look bad in front of Chancellor Grant because she had refused to sleep with him. What a fool she'd been! From her current vantage point, it was obvious Terry Wither-spoon had never been genuinely interested in her. Obviously, he'd seen her merely as an easy conquest—one last fling before his wife arrived.

Bertie kept to herself as much as possible for the rest of the day. Sooner or later, she would share her story with Ellen, perhaps over a few drinks at Rudy's Tap. But at the moment, the pain of Wither-spoon's betrayal was too raw to share with anyone. At that moment, all she wanted was to be left alone.

But before Bertie could crawl home to lick her wounds in solitude, she was going to have to tell her choir that their show had been can-celled. All week, she'd been relentlessly upbeat. Insisting that the lawsuit was a temporary obstacle, she'd assured the choir that the show they'd worked so hard to put together would, in fact, go on as scheduled. But now what would she tell them?

Bertie waited for her students to file into the classroom, then deliv-ered the bad news in plain, unvarnished language.

"The chancellor has decided to cancel our concert," she said.

For a moment, there was shocked silence in the room. Then Nyala Clark piped up from the back row.

"I thought the judge was going to stop this stupid lawsuit," she said in an injured voice. "You said so yourself."

"I did think that," Bertie said simply. "And I was right. The judge threw out Melissa's case. But apparently Mrs. Jones is going to ap-peal, and the chancellor is afraid the suit will drag on for several more months. Since the outcome of the case remains uncertain, he had no choice but to cancel the show."

The students stared glumly at Bertie for a long minute. Finally, Maurice Green spoke.

"This just ain't right. No way I'm ever gonna forgive Melissa this. Not if I live to be a hundred years old!"

TyJuana Barnes stood up and raised her fist in the air. "Somebody need to go over there and talk to that girl," she shouted. Bertie's star alto was built like a small tank and had the attitude to match. As she spoke, a defiant murmur of approval rippled through the group.

"That is absolutely out of the question," Bertie said firmly. "Other than our legal team, no one from the college is allowed to have any contact with Melissa."

"Yeah, well, that's you, Mrs. B," Maurice said, hiking up his jeans as he spoke. "I'm talking about a little unofficial contact. A friendly visit from her fellow students."

"Yeah," TyJuana said in a menacing tone. "We could drop by there tonight. All of us. Straighten her skanky little ass out. Show her the light."

"Do you want to go to jail?" Bertie looked out at her students with a challenging stare. "If any of you so much as sets a toe on Melissa Jones' property, her mother is going to have you arrested."

As Bertie's words hit home, her students slumped lower and lower in their seats. Like the air leaking from a punctured tire, she watched the energy drain from their faces. It didn't take a mind reader to know what they were thinking.

The concert was too good to be true. We should have known it would never really happen. Good things are just not in the cards for people like us.

When she got home from work that evening, Bertie marched straight into the kitchen and poured herself a double shot of brandy. She did not consider herself a heavy drinker, but tonight, a belt of the hard stuff was absolutely mandatory. As the liquor burned its way down her throat, Bertie dug through her CD collection until she found The O'Jays album she was looking for.

She put their vintage hit *Back Stabbers* on repeat and poured herself another drink. Sister Destina might not have gotten much else right, but she'd been accurate about one thing—Dr. Terrance Witherspoon had turned out to be very a false friend, indeed.

Chapter Twenty-Seven

When the doorbell rang half an hour later, Bertie dragged herself down the stairs on wobbly legs and squinted through the peephole. David Mackenzie stood on her front porch with his coat over his arm and a worried look on his face.

With a sigh, Bertie shot back the deadbolt and opened the door.

"Is that The O'Jays?" Mac said. "I sure hope you're not playing *Back Stabbers* on my account."

"Not at all, Mac." With an embarrassed shrug, Bertie led him upstairs to the living room and turned down her CD player. "But I should warn you, I won't be very good company. Metro College has cancelled my choir concert."

"I thought the judge turned down Fania Jones' request for a preliminary injunction," Mac said. "If that's the case, there should be no problem with you going ahead with the show."

"She's appealing his decision," Bertie said. "Not only that, but she's filed a Civil Rights case in federal court. She claims Melissa's right to free speech is being violated. She's suing the college for one hundred million dollars in punitive damages."

Mac snorted in disgust. "That is the most ridiculous thing I've ever heard. There is no way on God's green earth she's going to win."

"Tell that to Chancellor Grant," Bertie said. "The man hates controversy in any form. The thought that this case could drag on for months has got him totally spooked. So to be on the safe side, he's pulled the plug."

"Oh, Bertie. I am sorry. I know how long you've been working on that show."

"Three months down the drain," Bertie said bitterly. "And there's not a damn thing I can do about it."

"In that case, I'm especially glad I decided to stop by this evening," Mac said. He sat down next to Bertie on the couch and squeezed her arm sympathetically. "Sounds like you could use some company."

"It's been a lousy day, and that's a fact," Bertie said.

As the rest of the *Back Stabbers* album played softly in the background, she and Mac sat in silence for several minutes. Finally, Bertie turned to the lawyer and said, "What was it you wanted to see me about, anyway?"

"More bad news, I'm afraid," Mac replied. "I just came from the courthouse. Mabel Howard is being held on suspicion of murder."

Bertie sighed heavily. "Poor Mabel. How is she holding up?"

"She was really out of it at the hearing today. Her eyes were blank, and she could barely get up the energy to answer my questions. Judge Brenner has ordered her to undergo a full round of psychiatric tests."

"Mabel's always been a bit of a flake," Bertie said. "But I can't imagine her actually killing someone. What on earth was she doing with that sword in her hand, anyway?"

"She says Sweetwater was dead when she arrived at his office that night. The sword was lying across his body. When she bent down to see if there was anything she could do, she picked the weapon up without thinking."

Bertie nodded. "I thought so. The question is, do you believe her?"

"I would like to, Bertie. As her lawyer, it's my job to convince the judge that she's telling the truth, no matter what I believe."

Mac slumped wearily against the cushions on her living room couch. His suit was rumpled, his tie hung at a crooked angle, and there were dark circles under his eyes. As the lawyer spoke, Bertie couldn't help thinking he needed a woman to take care of him.

"I've been drinking brandy for the past hour," she said suddenly. "I think I could use a cup of coffee. Can I get you something?"

Mac smiled. "That would be terrific. I haven't had time to eat since breakfast."

Five minutes later, Bertie set two steaming mugs of black coffee and a tin of Danish butter cookies on the living room coffee table.

"It's not the healthiest of snacks, but it'll tide you over for a while," she said. "Do the police have any other suspects?"

"Other than Mabel, no," Mac said wearily, munching on a cookie. "Just between the two of us, I'd dearly love to see another credible subject enter the picture. I made a big deal in court today about the size differential between Mabel and the two murder victims. However, I neglected to mention that Mabel was the captain of her college fencing team. If the DA is worth his salt, he'll uncover that piece of evidence on his own in the next few days."

"You think he will?"

"It's only a matter of time," Mac said. "He's got an entire staff of research assistants whose sole mission in life is to convict Mabel Howard of first-degree murder."

Bertie sipped her coffee thoughtfully. "I read something in Sister Destina's thesis that might be helpful. Remember the Home Hoodoo Program?"

Mac nodded wearily. "That's the scam Mabel claimed that Sweetwater and Destina concocted to gobble up real estate at bargain basement prices. Trouble is, there's no proof the program ever existed. According to Mabel, Sweetwater kept a log of burned houses in his office safe. But the police have been over his office with a fine-tooth comb. No such books have been found."

"Of course not," Bertie said triumphantly. "The murderer took them."

"Unless they never existed. Unless they were just another one of Sister Destina's inventions."

"But Destina wrote about the program in her thesis," Bertie said.

"Described the whole thing and implicated both Jabarion and Sweet-water. Doesn't that substantiate Mabel's allegations?"

Mac shrugged. "Sister Destina is dead. Mabel can barely put together a coherent sentence. Jabarion could probably tell us more, but I'll need to get a court order before I can talk to him. Was there anything else about Mabel in this thesis thing?"

"I know I promised to read it," Bertie said sheepishly. "I stayed up reading till two in the morning the other night, but I fell asleep before I could finish it."

Mac sighed and looked at his watch. "This has been one hell of a day. Nearly seven o'clock, and I haven't even looked at any of my other cases."

"I'm almost done reading Destina's manuscript. If I read fast, I could probably finish it and send you a summary before Monday."

"That would be great," Mac said with a tired smile. He leaned over and kissed her lightly on the cheek. "You're the best, Bertie. One in a million."

Long after Mac had driven away, Bertie stood lost in thought by her front door. In the past ten days, she had been kissed by three different men—a thing that in and of itself was a source of considerable wonder. And although David Mackenzie was not as handsome as The Ace of Spades, or as suave as Terry Witherspoon, the lawyer had an indefinable presence, an aura of masculinity, that Bertie was beginning to find irresistible. Something about the assurance with which he carried himself, even in the midst of a major life crisis, resonated deep within Bertie's heart. And unlike The Ace or Terry Witherspoon, David Mackenzie was a man a girl could depend on, a man who honored his commitments. *Dependability is written all over him,* Bertie thought. Even in his dogged loyalty to a wife who, by all accounts, wasn't worthy to shine his shoes.

After Mac left, Bertie fixed herself a cup of tea and carried it up to her bedroom. Ten minutes later, she was once again immersed in Destina's magnum opus:

It is a well-known fact that the German mind is superior to that of most individuals, except, of course, for Jamaicans, who are the most superior of all. It is for this reason that I have made a special point to delve into the ontology and etymology of the German language.

After a digression of several pages, Bertie found a quote from the philosopher Friedrich Nietzsche written in bold font and positioned in the center of the page:

Man is something that shall be overcome.

Nietzsche had believed in a kind of superman, an "ubermensch." The ubermensch was superior to other humans. Because of this, he would not be bound by religion, conventional morality, or the law. Adolph Hitler had been a big fan.

On the next page, the German word for "attention" had been printed in large type.

ACHTUNG!

IT HAS BEEN REVEALED to me, Sister Destina the Ubermensch, that evildoers reside at 11872 S. Argyle Avenue! The foul stench of their doings against Kolab and Maly is known to the Almighty. Whilst in a dream state, an angel appeared and revealed the truth to me, Sister Destina the Ubermensch. **Evildoers BEWARE!** Your doings have been psychically perceived by me. Those responsible **WILL SUFFER** the mighty sword of retribution.
ALSO SPAKE DESTINA

Give me a break, Bertie thought wearily. Sister Destina's delusional ramblings were really beginning to get on her nerves. Thank goodness there were only a handful of pages left.

For the next ten pages, Destina railed against a host of so-called "enemies": the U.S. government, the IRS, the World Bank, and, to Bertie's surprise, the Gay Rights Movement. After taking a final pot-shot at the inequality of the Federal Tax Code, Sister Destina concluded her magnum opus on a Biblical note.

> The Angel of the Lord appeared to me last night. And lo, I have heard the Word from on high! I, Sister Destina, who thought herself an ubermensch, have been severely chastised. Things can no longer continue as they have been. I must clear my karmic field now, before it is too late.

Underneath this paragraph was a list of names:

Mabel Howard
Jabarion Coutze
Max Sweetwater
Penny Swift
Bertie Bigelow

As she read her name, Bertie felt the skin at the back of her neck begin to tingle. Destina had begged Bertie to come to her house the night she was killed. It was likely the psychic had extended a similar invitation to every person on this list.

But someone hadn't been interested in helping Sister Destina clear her karma.

Someone, possibly one of the people on this very list, had gone to the psychic's home that night with murder on their mind.

Chapter Twenty-Eight

SATURDAY, NOVEMBER 4—8:00 AM

Bertie woke up the next morning suffused with a sense of melancholy. Heavy gray clouds covered the sky and blocked out the sun. The wind blowing in from Lake Michigan picked up leaves, papers, and trash from the sidewalk and sent them scurrying into the street. Despite her best efforts, the fall season, which had begun with such excitement and optimism, was ending on a note of disappointment, disillusionment, and death. Bertie took a deep breath and pulled her terrycloth robe closer to ward off the chill that had settled over her.

Stop brooding, she told herself sternly. *What's done is done. There's nothing you can do about it now.* She could not fix the fact that Destina was dead or that Mabel was in jail. She could not fix the fact that Melissa's mother was suing the college or that her concert had been cancelled. However, she could prevent the leaves currently swirling around her small backyard from blowing all over the sidewalk.

Bertie pulled on her coat, picked up a broom, and stepped outside.

"Lovely mornin'," Pat O'Fallon sang out. As usual, she and her sister, Colleen, were busy at work beautifying their already spotless patch of yard next door. "Great day ta be gettin' the yard in order."

"I suppose," Bertie said glumly. "Such a chill in the air. Winter's on the way."

"Why of course it is," Colleen said. "Ya wouldn't want to mess with the divine order of the seasons, now would ya?"

155

"No, of course not." Bertie poked at a pile of leaves with her broom. "It's just that lately time seems to pass faster than ever."

Pat nodded. "Just wait until you get to my age, dear. Each year seems to last about a day."

"That's why it's important to keep yer chin up and yer step lively," Colleen chimed in. "Keep it positive. You know, like it says in the song."

With an impish grin, Pat began to sing. "Be positive. Keep it positive."

The two sisters were well into the second chorus before they noticed that Bertie was not singing along.

"You're lookin' downright peaked," Colleen said. "What ails ya, Bertie?"

"My concert with The Ace of Spades has been cancelled." As she swept the remaining leaves from the sidewalk, Bertie gave the two sisters an abridged version of the latest developments.

"What a terrible shame," Pat said. "Girls sending naked pictures. Lawsuits. They'd have never put up with this sort of thing at Holy Angels, eh, Collie?"

"Not a-tall," Colleen replied. "At the first sign a trouble, Sister Agnes would have sent a priest in to lay some holy water about."

"Holy water and a switch," Pat added dourly.

"Melissa Jones could use a good talking to, for certain," Bertie said. "But it's her mother that's the real problem. She's the one who's old enough to know better."

"There's got to be somethin' evil in a person ta make her persist in such a wrong-headed manner," Pat said, shaking her head. "Must a-been touched by Satan."

Bertie shifted uncomfortably. The two sisters were kind souls and well-meaning enough, in their way, but talk of people being "touched by Satan" had a tendency to make her nervous.

"I don't know if I can go that far," she said slowly. "To be honest, I think the woman's just got mental problems."

"Oh, the devil's a busy one, Bertie. You never know who he'll touch next." In a rare moment of agreement, the two sisters nodded their heads in unison as Pat ticked off a list of the world's woes. "Mass murderers. Serial rapists. Child molesters. Terrorists who'd just as soon kill ya as look at ya. The devil's a busy one. Unspeakable evil is everywhere you look these days."

"Did you just say 'unspeakable evil'?"

"That's about the size of it," Pat said gravely.

A chill that had nothing to do with the weather ran down Bertie's spine.

"Remember I told you about Sister Destina? The psychic who was murdered? She used that exact phrase to describe the activities going on in a house on Argyle Avenue. I was tempted to ignore it, but listening to you talk, I'm not so sure. There's just a slim chance Destina might have been on to something."

"Sure she was," Collie said. "A claim like that cries out to be investigated. What you'll be wantin' are the full particulars—who owns the house, who lives there, that sort a thing."

Bertie sighed. "Even if there is something to this, the truth is, I don't have time to wait in line at the Cook County Assessor's office. I suppose I could drive by the address, but unless I am willing to stake the place out twenty-four hours a day, I doubt I'd find out anything."

"No need for extreme measures," Pat said gaily. "No need at all. You can find everything you need to know right on the internet. Isn't that right, Collie?"

"Course it is," Colleen said. She leaned over the fence and put a pale, arthritic finger alongside her nose. "You can sleuth it out on the Web. Go to Intel.com."

Pat O'Fallon turned to her sister. "No, Collie, that's not it."

"Yes, it is," Collie said an in injured voice. "There ya go, pickin' at me again."

"I wouldn't have ta pick if ya'd use half the brains the Almighty put in yer skull," Pat snapped. "The website is called Intelligentsearch.

com." She spelled the letters out in a careful schoolmarm's voice. "If you go there, you'll get to the bottom of this thing, for sure."

Bertie shook her head in amazement. "How on earth did you two find out about that stuff?"

Pat grinned impishly. "We may be old, but we're not in the grave just yet, you know." Rolling up her sleeve, she stuck out her arm to display the shiny Apple Watch strapped to her bony wrist. "My nephew Harry keeps us up to date on all the latest gadgets. It wouldn't do to get behind the times, now would it, Bertie?"

Later that afternoon, Bertie fixed herself a cup of tea, fired up her laptop, and punched the Argyle Avenue address into the search engine at Intelligentsearch.com. Sure enough, for a small fee, the website promised to provide her with the name of the house's owner and current residents.

As she waited for the page to load, Bertie made a conscious effort to keep her expectations low. In the course of her so-called thesis, Sister Destina had used the term "unspeakable evil" to describe a laundry list of pet peeves, including the Pope, Congress, the CIA, and the American Library Association. It was likely the Argyle Avenue reference would turn out to be yet another wild goose chase.

As the image slowly materialized on her computer screen, Bertie put down her teacup and leaned in for a closer look.

> 11872 S. Argyle Avenue
> Type of building: Condominium unit
> Number of rooms: 5
> Owner of record: Leroy T. Jefferson – 5744 S. Prairie Ave.,
> Chicago, IL 60619
> Date of last purchase: May 24, 2012
> Purchase price: $75,000
> Phone: none

As she read and reread the entry, Bertie's mind whirled in circles. The man who owned the home Sister Destina had written about was Leroy T. Jefferson, the head of the Chicago Zoning Board and the very man who'd been poisoned in Charley Howard's restaurant. Surely this was no accident.

Pondering this remarkable information put Bertie so deep in thought that she almost didn't hear her cell phone ringing. Marvin Gaye was well into the third repetition of the tag line from "What's Goin' On" before she answered.

Penny Swift's nasal twang had an injured quality. "I was beginning to think you were ignoring my call, Bertie."

"Goodness no," Bertie replied hastily. "I was just distracted, that's all."

"Well, you are going to be very glad you picked up when you hear what I have to say." Penny cleared her throat. "The Kenilworth Community Club is having a special Diversity Banquet next Sunday. I'd like you to attend as my guest."

It was a good thing for race relations that Penny Swift could not see the expression on Bertie's face. Until the 1950s, blacks had been legally barred from living in Kenilworth. And in 1964, an angry crowd had burned a cross on the lawn of the one black family brave enough to move there. Even now, Bertie would have been very surprised if the village had more than ten African-American residents.

Imbued with a sense of mission, Penny Swift plowed ahead. "Kenilworth is making great strides, Bertie. This is the first time we've ever had an event of this nature. I'd been planning to invite Destina, but of course, that's no longer possible."

When Bertie didn't respond right away, Penny sighed. "I miss going out to the South Side," she said wistfully. "Sister Destina was totally unique. I don't know where I'll ever find another spiritual advisor like her."

"Have you heard from any of her regulars recently?" Bertie said.

"As a matter of fact, I have. Jabarion Coutze called me over the weekend. Went to some kind of conference in St. Louis and came back all fired up. He wants to start a hip-hop clothing business. He asked me if my husband might be willing to stake him a few dollars."

Not bloody likely, Bertie thought to herself. From what she'd heard about Penny's wayward husband, he did not strike her as the philanthropic type.

"What did your husband say?"

"In a nutshell? No way, no how," Penny said bitterly. "Morgan can be a real prick sometimes. Sister Destina always used to say he was sleeping with that pea-brained secretary of his."

"Did you believe her?"

"I did at the time," Penny said. "Now I don't know what to believe. Sister Destina lied to me, Bertie. The day she died, she insisted I come over so she could make a clean breast of things."

Struggling to keep the excitement out of her voice, Bertie said, "Did you say you were at Sister Destina's home on the night of the murder?"

Until that moment, Penny's tone had been breezy and intimate, but suddenly there was an edge to her voice. "Are you interrogating me, Bertie?"

"Of course not," Bertie said, backpedaling furiously. "I was just curious, that's all."

"I don't think I believe you," Penny said. "You want to know what I think? I think you're trying to dig up some dirt on me. Something that will divert suspicion from Mabel Howard."

"Mabel is my friend," Bertie said in what she hoped was a placating tone. "Quite naturally, I'm trying to help her. If you were at Sister Destina's that night, you may have seen or heard something that could be important."

"What I did or did not do that night is none of your business," Penny said curtly. "The more I think about it, I do not think I want a snoop like you coming anywhere near my Diversity Banquet."

As the phone connection went dead, Bertie laughed out loud for the first time in two days. *Wait till I tell Ellen about this,* she thought. But first, she needed to call Mac and let him know what she had learned—both about Penny's probable visit to Sister Destina's home the night of the murder and about the Argyle Avenue property owned by Commissioner Leroy Jefferson.

Should she call Mac on his cell phone? Since it was now late in the afternoon on a Saturday, she decided to try calling the lawyer at home.

As she waited for Mac to pick up, Bertie smiled in anticipation. They'd had a lovely conversation last night. Surely, the new information she'd discovered would merit another in-depth conversation. Perhaps they could get together for dinner later that evening.

"Who the hell is this?" Angelique Mackenzie's voice snapped Bertie out of her reverie. "David's busy right now. He'll have to get back to you later."

In a state of shock and guilty embarrassment for the amorous thoughts she'd been harboring, Bertie mumbled a reply and beat a hasty retreat. For the second time in as many weeks, she felt like a total fool. Mac had given her the impression his wife had moved out, that she'd gone to live with another man. But apparently, Angie Mackenzie was back and sounding every inch the lady of the house.

Bertie had been a fool to get her hopes up. She knew that now, but one thing was certain. It would never happen again. Not ever. She did not need Mac or any other man in her life, thank you very much. If Mac wasn't going to help her investigate the murders, Bertie Bigelow was fully capable of handling matters on her own.

Brushing away a tear, Bertie marched upstairs and fired up her laptop. A quick visit to the CookCounty.gov website showed that Commissioner Leroy T. Jefferson held a town hall meeting at the East Washington Park Community Center on the first Monday of every month. On Monday, she would attend the meeting and ask for a few minutes of his time. Now that she'd thought of it, Bertie wondered why the idea had not occurred to her before. If she wanted to find out about Commissioner Jefferson's second house, she would simply ask him.

Chapter Twenty-Nine

As Bertie Bigelow drove west on Garfield Boulevard, she hoped that Commissioner Jefferson's town hall meeting would not turn out to be a total waste of time. This time last week, she would have called Mac to get his opinion. But the way Bertie felt at the moment, she was damned if she'd ever speak to the burly lawyer again. After finding a parking space, she locked her car and walked down the brightly lit street, past a large vacant lot and a bustling McDonald's, to the low-rise brick building that housed the East Washington Park Community Center.

To Bertie's surprise, the place was packed. She'd been expecting a lightly attended and entirely perfunctory Q&A session, attended by a few bored retirees and maybe a wino or two looking to come in out of the cold. But every seat in the room was taken. As she found a place leaning against the wall to the right of the speaker's platform, Commissioner Leroy Jefferson was being introduced by Alderman Gregg Mathers. With his round belly and small head, the alderman reminded Bertie of a bowling pin with arms.

"My fellow Chicagoans," Mathers said. His voice was that of the quintessential South Side politician—deep, stentorian, and touched with a hint of the Deep South. "As you know, the Gilded Lily Development Company is planning to erect a highrise building in our neighborhood."

A tiny gray-haired woman wearing a Sunday-go-to-meeting hat and a pair of white gloves stood and shook her fist at the platform.

"Send those vultures back downtown," she shouted in a surprisingly penetrating voice. "They're trying to take over our neighborhood."

There was a roar of assent from the crowd.

The alderman smiled like a teacher indulging a bright but unruly pupil. "We all understand your position, Mrs. Crawford. Please take your seat and allow Commissioner Jefferson to answer your questions."

Muttering to herself, the woman returned to her seat, and the alderman resumed his presentation.

"Ladies and gentlemen, I present to you a man who needs no introduction here in Washington Park. For years, he's been a champion of neighborhood advocacy. He's a member of the Washington Park Commerce Association, a deacon at Blessed Savior Episcopal Church, and the founder of the Preserve Our Community Task Force." Mathers paused to permit a smattering of polite applause. "Tonight, I see the commissioner is accompanied by his lovely wife, Alvitra." He nodded toward a massive woman, who sat tapping her foot impatiently in the front row.

In spite of the expensive jewelry and designer suit she wore, Mrs. Jefferson's build and jowly face reminded Bertie of an out of shape sumo wrestler. Like Queen Elizabeth acknowledging her subjects, Alvitra Jefferson nodded and graced the audience with a small wave.

"For those of you who don't know, Alvitra's father was the great H. L. R. Swade, founder of the Swade Insurance Group. You don't get any more Washington Park than this family, ladies and gentlemen. Please join me in welcoming Commissioner Leroy T. Jefferson."

The crowd applauded as Jefferson—wearing a tan Brooks Brothers suit, a white shirt, gleaming black patent leather shoes, and a maroon bow tie—took his place at the podium.

"My fellow Chicagoans," he said in a clipped, precise voice that could have belonged to an Oxford University graduate. "Our beautiful South Side oasis has been hit by a crisis in recent months."

"You got that right," Mrs. Crawford chimed in loudly. "Question is, what are *you* going to do about it?"

The crowd, which had been sitting patiently through Jefferson's introductory remarks, began to mutter among themselves.

"She's right," a gray-haired man shouted from the back row. "We all know what the problem is. Developers from downtown looking to move up here, drive up prices, and push us out of our homes."

"When they tore down the projects on State Street, this whole area became a battle zone." Mrs. Crawford was standing now, waving her gloved hands for emphasis. "People got displaced. New gangs moved in. But we pulled together as a community and closed ranks against outside troublemakers. We've still got a long way to go, but we're determined to preserve our neighborhood. And we are not about to be driven from our homes by Max Sweetwater and a bunch of eggheads from the U of C."

Commissioner Jefferson nodded. "I've travelled all over the world," he said grandly. "And I've seen what unchecked development has done in cities like Bangkok and Manila. I am here to assure you that no highrise development will take place along Fifty-Ninth Street. Washington Park's unique residential character will remain unchanged."

Although the crowd applauded dutifully, Mrs. Crawford's face retained its skeptical expression. "We've heard all this before," she said bluntly. "Meanwhile, the U of C has bought two more lots on Garfield Boulevard. Real estate sharks are grabbing up property here like there's no tomorrow, Commissioner. Sweetwater's dead, but his tower at Fifty-Ninth and Wabash is alive and well."

Emboldened by Mrs. Crawford's feistiness, a thin man in a dark leather jacket chimed in. "She's right, Commissioner. They are going right ahead with plans to demolish all the homes on that block."

"Not for long," Jefferson said grimly. "As the head of the Chicago Zoning Board of Appeal, I have a lot of clout in this city. I promise you people that I intend to do everything in my power to preserve this neighborhood. Contrary to popular opinion, the University of Chicago does not own this town. Neither do the corporate interests downtown."

"Amen!" Mrs. Crawford shouted as the crowd applauded wildly.

Bertie had thought that this would just be a rather dull meeting about zoning concerns or some such. She had even come up with some questions to ask. But given the fervent temper of the proceedings, her question about the potholes on Prairie Avenue now seemed inappropriate. As she wracked her brain to come up with a more pertinent line of inquiry, Commissioner Jefferson stretched his arms wide in benediction.

"I am a student of the blues, ladies and gentlemen. It is black America's finest and most powerful poetic statement. I'd like to dedicate this song to my friends at Gilded Lily Development."

Jefferson spread his legs, took a deep breath, and began to sing in a surprisingly rich tenor:

> Everybody's got to pay the piper some time
> Oh yes they do.
> Everybody's got to pay the piper some time.
> You may be ridin' high, babe
> Got the world tied up in string.
> You may be lookin good, babe
> But when that piper comes to call
> Your looks won't mean a thing.
> Everybody's got to pay the piper some time.

As the crowd applauded wildly, the commissioner took a bow and stepped back from the podium.

"Thank you, ladies and gentlemen," Alderman Mathers said. "That concludes our meeting for this week. Keep on keepin' on!"

As the crowd began to head outside, Commissioner Jefferson stepped off the speaker's platform.

"Excuse me, Commissioner," Bertie said as she hurried toward the stage. As Jefferson turned to face her, she continued, "My name is Bertie Bigelow. I'd like to ask you some questions about a mutual friend."

The commissioner, still emanating a messianic glow in the wake of his triumphant speech, nodded distractedly. "A mutual friend, you say?" He extracted a monogrammed lace handkerchief from his breast pocket and daubed the sweat from his brow. "And who might that be?"

When Bertie mentioned Sister Destina's name, Jefferson turned pale. "That woman had me poisoned," he snapped. "She's no friend of mine." As he began to walk away, Bertie surprised them both by grabbing Jefferson's arm.

"Please, Commissioner," she said. "It's important. Is there somewhere we can talk?"

Bertie fully expected him to pull away and stride off into the crowd. Instead, the commissioner hesitated. "What did you say your name was?"

"Bertie Bigelow. As you know, Sister Destina has been murdered. I'm investigating the killing on behalf of my client, Mabel Howard."

"Charley's wife?" Was Bertie mistaken, or had an expression of panic passed across the commissioner's face? "What did she say about me?"

Gotcha, Bertie thought to herself. "It isn't so much what Mabel says as what Sister Destina herself had to say before she died. Do you own a house at 11872 Argyle Avenue?"

Jefferson's eyes narrowed. "This is neither the time nor the place to discuss this matter."

"Why not, Commissioner?"

Bertie surprised herself again by standing directly in Jefferson's path. Either the man was going to knock her over or he was going to have to answer her question. Just as it appeared Jefferson was going to utilize the former alternative, Alvitra Jefferson materialized at his side.

"I don't believe I've had the pleasure," Alvitra said smoothly. "When I was a little girl, my daddy used to always take me around the community and introduce me to his clients." She placed a proprietary hand on the commissioner's shoulder. "I always like to meet my husband's acquaintances."

If Leroy T. Jefferson was relieved to see his wife, he did not show it. If anything, Bertie thought the commissioner looked even more nervous.

"This woman is not an acquaintance, in the true sense of the word," he harrumphed, shooting a pleading glance in Bertie's direction. "I am meeting her for the first time just now. I am sure we can resolve the real estate matter you mentioned, Mrs. Bigelow," Jefferson said. "In fact, I believe I have some time available tomorrow evening. Call my secretary, and I'll have him set up the appointment."

As Jefferson shuffled through his pockets and handed Bertie a business card, Alvitra never released her talon-like grip on his shoulder.

"Come, Leroy. There are other constituents waiting to speak with you." With a cool nod, Alvitra Jefferson took her husband's arm and steered him in the opposite direction.

No question who wears the pants in that family, Bertie thought to herself. It was almost as if Alvitra suspected her husband of having an affair. The woman was emanating that same kind of suspicious, patrol-the-borders energy. Not that Jefferson seemed like the wandering type. Despite his rich tenor voice and love for the blues, the commissioner struck Bertie as a tedious, nitpicking fuddy-duddy who'd be unlikely to stray too far from home.

Chapter Thirty

At the stroke of nine the following morning, Bertie dug through her purse until she found Commissioner Jefferson's business card. Two minutes later, his personal secretary was on the line.

"Yes, Mrs. Bigelow. I've been expecting your call. The commissioner will see you in his office this evening at seven p.m. Is that convenient?"

Feeling the glow of accomplishment, Bertie stopped by the faculty lounge for a celebratory cup of coffee. Professor George Frayley, chairman of the Metro College Events Committee and Ellen Simpson's personal nemesis, was holding court in the corner with his back to the door.

"Popular music has no place in a serious college curriculum," he said in his patrician New England accent. "Mrs. Jones' lawsuit is a terrible thing, of course. But in the end, it will lead to a positive result, both for us and for our students."

Maria Francione, dressed in a tight-fitting leotard top and a wide cotton skirt, shook her head. "Don't be ridiculous, George," she said, waving her hands in the air for emphasis. "Bertie was completely within her rights throwing Melissa out of her choir. If the little *puttana* had tried a stunt like that in my drama class, I'd have done the same thing. And now her mother's suing the college? Give me a break!"

Jack Iverson peered over the top of his *New York Times* and nodded. "Maria's right. A teacher should have a right to control her classroom. I'm all for civil liberties. It's what I teach, after all. But things have gotten way out of hand."

As the college's most senior faculty member, Iverson was accustomed to having the last word on any campus controversy. But George Frayley, who was the second most senior faculty member, showed no sign of backing down.

"Pandering to the lowest common denominator always gets you in trouble," Frayley sniffed. "If Professor Bigelow had kept her student's minds on the classics, the sexting episode would never have occurred."

Bertie had remained silent so far. George Frayley's opinion was not going to affect the outcome of Fania Jones' lawsuit in the least. Still, his comments rankled.

"The Metro College Madrigal Singers took first place in the Illinois State Choir Competition last year," Bertie announced loudly. "Not third place. Not second place. First place!"

George Frayley had been standing with his back to the door and had not seen Bertie come in. Embarrassed at the realization that she had probably overheard his entire diatribe, he fell silent.

"The choir sang *Vestiva i colli* by Giovanni Palestrina," Bertie said. "One of the best known madrigals of the Italian Renaissance. My students are not dummies, George. They can and do sing anything that is put in front of them, from Bach to rock."

Bertie picked up her coffee and stomped back to her office. Slamming the door loudly behind her, she sighed wearily. This was shaping up to be the worst semester of her life. Mabel was in jail. Her concert had been cancelled, and her love life was in the toilet. There had to be something she could do about at least one of those problems.

Frustrated, she paced the length of the room. Six steps to the bookcase overflowing with CDs, musical scores, and old textbooks. Reverse direction. Six steps past her battered metal desk to the coat rack by the door. As she passed her desk for the tenth time, Bertie stopped short.

It did not take a rocket scientist to see that Fania Jones was determined to prevent the Metro College Singers from performing with The Ace of Spades, at any cost. But what if they were to perform without The Ace? What if Metro College was not the sponsor?

Two hours later, Bertie walked into choir practice and told her students she had an important announcement to make.

"We have been invited to perform at the South Side Museum for their annual fundraiser," she said.

Maurice Green's face was a study in skepticism. "You makin' this up, Mrs. B?"

"No, I am not," Bertie said firmly. It broke her heart to see how cynical her students had become in the wake of recent events. "I spoke to the museum director this morning. She's an old friend of mine. She wants us to be part of the opening ceremony."

Nyala Clark raised her hand. "You talking about the fancy dress ball that's on Channel Nine every year?"

Bertie nodded. "The Kwanzaa KickStart is a huge event. The opening ceremony will be broadcast live on WGN-TV. Unfortunately, The Ace will not be performing with us, but Dwyane Wade will be in the audience."

Maurice Green's eyes widened. "D-Wade? From the Bulls?"

"The very same," Bertie said with a smile.

"But what about the lawsuit?" TyJuana Barnes said. "Isn't there some kind of legal paper saying we can't do our show?"

"I spoke to Chancellor Grant this morning," Bertie said. "He's going to check with our lawyers. But as long as The Ace is not involved, he doesn't think there will be a problem."

As she spoke, Bertie sensed an air of cautious optimism fill the room.

"The important thing is not to give up hope," she said firmly. "We've worked too hard to quit now."

Chapter Thirty-One

Tuesday, November 7—5:30 PM

Bertie returned home with a satisfied smile on her face. Although her students were not yet jumping with joy about the concert she'd proposed, the tide was definitely turning.

Sadly, the same could not be said for her sleuthing activities. Mac had yelled at her. Charley Howard had fired her. Worse still, Mabel Howard was now the prime suspect in two grisly murders.

Despite her lack of tangible success, Bertie was too stubborn to give up. She had resolved one pressing issue. If she put her mind to it, perhaps she'd be able to figure out a solution to the murder investigation as well. She brewed herself a cup of tea, dug out a sheet of paper and a pen, and sat down at her kitchen table to write.

POSSIBLE SUSPECTS

1—Max Sweetwater

He and Destina had been business partners. If their relationship had gone sour, it was easy to imagine him killing the psychic. But why had Sweetwater been killed? If the real estate mogul had enemies outside Destina's inner circle, finding his killer would require resources Bertie could not possibly muster. She decided to stick with the theory that he and Sister Destina had been killed by the same person, at least for now.

2—Penny Swift

Despite her designer clothing, buff body, and up-market lifestyle, Penny Swift was a deeply unhappy woman. Her husband was cheating on her, and she'd been betrayed by Sister Destina, the one person on earth she'd thought she could trust. But why would Penny have wanted to kill Max Sweetwater? Had she invested in his Wabash Towers project? Bertie made a note to ask Mac if he'd uncovered any information about that.

3—Jabarion Coutze

The boy was an obvious suspect. His father was a notorious criminal. He'd even admitted to setting fires as a part of Destina's Home Hoodoo program. But was he capable of murder?

4—Charley Howard

Given all the trouble Sister Destina had caused him, it was easy to imagine the Hot Sauce King stabbing her in a violent fit of temper. But Charley would have had no motive for killing Max Sweetwater. From what Bertie could tell, the two men barely knew each other. But what if the developer had threatened Mabel in some way? Under those circumstances, there was no telling what Charley might do.

5—Mabel Howard

Much as she hated to do it, Bertie could not omit her friend from the list of suspects. She'd been in Sister Destina's home the night of the murder. She'd been caught standing over Sweetwater's dead body with a bloody sword in her hand. Could the sweet, slightly daffy woman Bertie thought she knew be a cold-blooded killer?

With a sigh of frustration, Bertie put down her pen and checked her watch. To her surprise, the time had flown. It was now nearly six fifteen. She would have to hurry if she wanted to get downtown in time for her seven o'clock meeting with Commissioner Jefferson.

As she was walking out the door, the wall phone in her kitchen rang.

"Thank God you picked up!" Mabel Howard sounded even more breathless than usual. "My spirit guides told me to call you immediately."

"Where are you?" Bertie said. She knew Mabel was supposed to be undergoing evaluation at Northwestern University's Psychiatric Center. "Please tell me you haven't run away from the hospital."

"Of course not," Mabel said. "I was able to persuade this lovely nurse to let me make a phone call. I told her it was an absolute emergency."

Bertie glanced at her watch—six twenty. Although she wanted to help Mabel with her latest emergency, she felt she'd be doing her friend a bigger service by not missing her meeting with Commissioner Jefferson.

"It's good to hear your voice," Bertie said. "But I can't talk right now. I'm on my way out the door."

"You're going out?" Mabel's already high-pitched voice jumped up another octave. "Oh no, Bertie. You can't do that!"

"Why on earth not?"

Mabel took a deep breath. "Since Sister Destina died, I've been getting messages. A voice speaks to me, tells me things."

"You've been under a lot of strain lately," Bertie said in what she hoped was a calming tone of voice. "Perhaps you should lie down and rest."

"You don't believe me," Mabel said sadly. "Nevertheless, my guidance was clear. You need to stay indoors for the next ten days."

"How am I supposed to do that?" Bertie said. "I've got to go to work, you know."

"Okay, I get that, but don't go out unnecessarily. And *especially* don't go out at night. That's the most dangerous time of all."

Bertie shook her head sadly. "Get some rest, Mabel. Mac and I are doing everything we can to help you beat this thing. Meanwhile, do what the doctors tell you, and please try to stay out of trouble."

Perhaps Mac would be better off building an insanity defense, Bertie thought as she pulled on her coat and stepped outside. Mabel Howard had gone completely 'round the bend.

Chapter Thirty-Two

The zoning board was located downtown in a large modern tower at the north end of the Loop. In normal circumstances, it would have taken Bertie no more than forty-five minutes to get there, but at that time of the night, traffic was terrible. Worse still, she had to circle the block three times before she was able to find a parking space.

The reception room was empty by the time Bertie walked into Commissioner Jefferson's office. No one manned the two large desks positioned at the front of the room, and no one sat in the row of leather-backed wooden chairs along the wall.

Muttering under her breath, Bertie checked her watch. It was now seven thirty. She was half an hour late, but perhaps the commissioner had not yet left for the day.

"Hello," Bertie called out. "I have an appointment to see Commissioner Jefferson. Is anyone here?"

She continued to call out as she stepped around the receptionist's station and walked past the rows of empty cubicles, but all she heard in reply was the sound of her heels clicking against the polished marble floor.

Just as she was about to give up, Commissioner Leroy T. Jefferson—wearing a tan three-piece suit, tasseled loafers, and a pink bowtie—emerged from a door at the end of the corridor.

174

"Ah! There you are, Mrs. Bigelow. I was afraid you were not going to be joining me this evening."

"I'm sorry to be so late," Bertie said. "Traffic was terrible on the Outer Drive."

"These things happen," the commissioner said grandly, holding open the door to his office. "The important thing is that you are here. Please come in."

As a teacher of singers, Bertie couldn't help but notice Jefferson's flawless diction. *It's downright uncanny,* she thought. *Almost like listening to a machine.*

A large oak desk dominated the room. The wall behind it was lined with the pictures of previous zoning commissioners—beefy men of power with broad smiles and shiny suits. To the right of the desk, a set of glass bookshelves held pictures of Jefferson, his hulking wife Alvitra, and their two pudgy children. To the left, a Japanese samurai sword in a decorative lacquer scabbard hung suspended from a hook on the wall.

Commissioner Jefferson closed the door and lowered himself delicately into the leather chair behind his desk. "Make yourself comfortable," he said and gestured toward the armchair across the desk from him.

"Will your assistant be joining us? Your secretary indicated that he would be present."

"I'm afraid my secretary misspoke, Mrs. Bigelow. There will be only two of us this evening. I hope that's all right."

It was definitely not what Bertie had expected. But unless she was willing to walk out of the meeting, there was nothing she could do about it. Taking her seat, she put her handbag in her lap, clasped her hands over it, and smiled.

"I'm sure you must be very busy," she said. "I appreciate your taking the time to see me."

"About the psychic you mentioned last night," Jefferson said. "This Sister Destina person. Can you tell me anything more?"

"I don't know much more than you do," Bertie said. "Sister Destina was running a protection racket. She gave one of your interns two hundred dollars to sprinkle rotten meat in your food. She knew that, if you got sick in Charley's restaurant, the place would be shut down immediately."

The commissioner steepled his fingers and studied her thoughtfully. "And this Destina person told you I owned property on Argyle Avenue?"

Bertie nodded. "She wrote about it in a document she mailed to me the day before she died."

"Destina must have been mistaken," Jefferson said in his high, precise voice. "More likely, it was a deliberate lie. The crazy he-she had already tried to kill me."

The commissioner had a point. Given all the other nonsense in Destina's thesis, the "unspeakable evil" at Argyle Avenue might just be another paranoid fantasy. But Bertie had a hunch. An intuition that, in spite of his prim language and self-righteous demeanor, Commissioner Leroy T. Jefferson was hiding something.

"Destina was working for Max Sweetwater," she said. "Perhaps he told her about your property."

"Sweetwater knew nothing about me." Pursing his lips disapprovingly, the commissioner leaned forward in his seat. "The man was a loathsome opportunist. He sucked our community dry in order to line his pockets. His death was tragic, of course. But at the risk of sounding callous, I think he got what he deserved."

"Your antipathy appears to have been reciprocated," Bertie said mildly. "Sweetwater referred to you as a 'rule-bound paper-pusher.'"

"Point taken," Jefferson said with a thin smile. "Are you familiar with the Washington Park area?"

"I live in Hyde Park. Just a couple of miles away."

"A couple of miles and at least five income brackets," Jefferson said tartly. "Believe me, Mrs. Bigelow, Max Sweetwater's so-called development company is the worst thing to happen to Washington Park in years."

"Perhaps," Bertie said. "But what does any of this have to do with Sister Destina? Argyle Avenue is nowhere near Washington Park. Can you explain why she would refer to your property as a place of 'unspeakable evil'?"

"The woman was a complete and total fraud. She wasn't even a real woman. Surely, you're not going to believe anything she had to say."

"But you *do* own a condo on Argyle Avenue," Bertie said. "It's a matter of public record. I looked up the deed myself."

"You don't understand," Jefferson said softly. "My wife doesn't know about the Argyle Avenue condo. There'd be hell to pay if she found out."

Surprised at the commissioner's swift change from pompous bureaucrat to terrified husband, Bertie decided to press her advantage. "Who are Kolab and Maly? Do they live there?"

Jefferson's eyes narrowed. "Where did you get those names?"

"The more relevant question is, where did Sister Destina get them?"

"I do not appreciate people poking around in my private affairs. Kolab and Maly are none of your damn business."

"But Sister Destina made it her business. Didn't she, Commissioner? Was she blackmailing you?"

Jefferson's mouth tightened in a grim line. "You are making a big mistake, Mrs. Bigelow. Don't push your luck with me."

Confident that she now had the commissioner on the run, Bertie was about to ask her next question when something silver caught her eye. For a moment, her brain failed to comprehend the meaning of the strange object. But then time stopped.

Commissioner Leroy T. Jefferson was holding a revolver in his right hand.

"My attorney is aware of my whereabouts," Bertie said, struggling to keep her voice steady. It was a lie, of course, but perhaps Jefferson wouldn't realize it. "If I do not return home by nine o'clock, he will call the police."

Jefferson studied Bertie across his desk for a long moment without speaking. "No, Mrs. Bigelow. No one knows you're here. You're the only one who's discovered my little secret."

"Put the gun down," Bertie said quietly. "I won't tell your wife about your second home. I promise."

Jefferson leaned back in his chair and looked up at the ceiling. While he considered her proposal, Bertie clutched her purse and shifted to the edge of her seat. If the commissioner could be distracted for even one minute, she might be able to escape. The door to the outside corridor was directly behind her and only six feet away.

As if he had read her mind, Jefferson sat erect and steadied the gun with both hands.

"I'm afraid it is far too late for negotiation," he said. "However, I am a generous man. Before you die, I am going to tell you a story. Have you ever been to Thailand?"

Bertie shook her head. Though her heart was hammering against her ribcage, it would not be wise to let the commissioner see how frightened she was. As though making polite conversation at a dinner party, she said, "I hear it's a beautiful country. I've always wanted to go there."

"The women in Thailand are nothing like the pushy broads you find over here. Thai women know how to make a man feel like a king. Especially the young ones."

"Are Kolab and Maly from Thailand?" Bertie asked, starting to put the pieces together.

"They came from Cambodia originally," Jefferson said. "And now they are mine. Two beautiful virgin brides, each just twelve years old."

"Virgin brides?" Bertie felt a rush of anger. "Those girls are far too young to be anybody's bride. What you are doing is wrong, Commissioner. Surely you can see that."

"Think you can stop me? I am a king, Mrs. Bigelow. The King of Argyle Avenue. No one is going to keep me from enjoying my little peaches. Not the immigration authorities. Not my gold-digging shrew of a wife. And certainly not a nosey bitch like you." The commissioner eyed her coldly. "I have to say, I've never shot anyone before. I'm much better with a sword. But I doubt you'd hold still long enough for me to retrieve my weapon of choice from the wall."

Bertie willed herself to stay calm. "Is that how you killed Sister Destina? With a sword?"

"What else could I do? She'd had some kind of prophetic vision. She called to say she'd been watching my condo for weeks, that she knew all about Kolab and Maly. She demanded I come out to the house to see her. She even threatened to tell the police." The commissioner smiled thinly. "I've been collecting swords for years, but I never thought I'd actually get to use one."

As Bertie sat clutching her purse, she realized that Commissioner Leroy T. Jefferson was stark raving crazy. At this point, her only hope was to keep him talking.

"There was music playing on the CD player when I got there," she said.

"A nice touch of staging, don't you agree? If there had been time, I would have selected music for Sweetwater's chastisement as well. 'Can't Buy Me Love' by the Beatles might have been nice. But I had to be quick. I could already hear Mabel Howard moving around in the main office."

"But why did you kill him?" Bertie said. "What did Max Sweetwater ever do to hurt you?"

"I did the world a service, removing that greedy bastard from the planet. The man was a pox on society. When Sweetwater realized I was not going to allow the commission to approve his monstrous tower on

Wabash Avenue, he went berserk. The man actually slapped me. Me, Leroy T. Jefferson, the King of Argyle Avenue! He really shouldn't have done that. Not in his office late at night with no one else around. And especially not with that fancy samurai sword hanging within easy reach. I mean really, Mrs. Bigelow. What would you have done if someone had disrespected you like that?"

"But I'm not being disrespectful," Bertie said. "There is absolutely no reason in the world for you to kill me. What will Kolab and Maly do if you get caught? Your virgin brides will be orphaned with no one to take care of them. Surely, you wouldn't want that to happen?"

"Nice try, Mrs. Bigelow," Jefferson said with a thin smile. "But you and I both know that, if I let you live, you'll go straight to the police. I can see it in your eyes."

"I would never do that," Bertie said, arranging her face in the most guileless expression she could muster. "You can trust me."

"Tisk tisk, Mrs. Bigelow. Don't you know lying is a sin?" Jefferson's egg-shaped face twisted in an ugly leer. "Didn't your mother teach you anything? You remind me of my lovely wife, Alvitra. Have I told you about her?"

"I met her at the meeting last night," Bertie said. "Is that her picture on the shelf behind you? She's lovely."

Jefferson's laugh was as humorless and dry as sandpaper. "Let me enlighten you, Mrs. Bigelow. My wife is a stupid, petty, materialistic pea brain. If Saks Fifth Avenue were to close tomorrow, her life would end. I only married Alvitra because her daddy was rich."

"How fascinating," Bertie said. Noticing that Jefferson had lowered his gun slightly, she gave an encouraging nod. If she could keep Jefferson talking long enough, perhaps she could persuade him to put away his gun. "So you got your start in Chicago political circles when you married Alvitra?"

"So I did," Jefferson said. "But once I became commissioner, I no longer needed her. I was a big man in my own right. And do you think my wife ever acknowledged my achievements?"

"I'm sure she did," Bertie said gently.

"For a college professor, you are awfully stupid," Jefferson snapped. "To this day, Alvitra treats me like a retarded ten-year-old. She orders me around, yells at me as if I were deaf. She gives me no respect, Mrs. Bigelow. No respect at all." Suddenly, the commissioner whirled and fired a bullet into his wife's picture on the shelf next to his desk. As the glass exploded and splinters flew, Bertie flinched in terror.

"Damn, that feels good," he said. The commissioner's jubilant grin was horrifying. "I was a little concerned about using the gun, but I needn't have worried. Killing you is going to be fun."

"But you haven't finished your story," Bertie said. If anyone else was working late in the zoning office, they would have heard the gunshots. Perhaps someone was hurrying down the hallway to investigate that very moment. "You told me about your wife, but you haven't told me about how you met Maly and Kolab."

Jefferson's expression softened. "Yes. You should learn about my beautiful flower children before you die. It's been hard keeping that secret. It truly has. Every time I'm sitting in a meeting. Every time my pea-brained wife harangues me. Every time one of my tiresome constituents starts a new complaint, I smile inside. Why? Because I know I have a secret identity. I may look like just another bureaucrat, but on Argyle Avenue, I am a king. Do you hear me? What I say goes. No arguments, no talking back. My word is law in my kingdom, Mrs. Bigelow. Law."

I bet it is, Bertie thought grimly. Two young girls, trapped in a foreign country over eight thousand miles from home, were not in a position to complain about much of anything.

"How did you get the girls over here in the first place?"

Jefferson waved a dismissive hand. "That was the easy part. There are plenty of folks in Asia just hungry enough to sell their children. Maly and Kolab were a bargain, in fact. Even with airfare, they cost me less than fifty grand, the both of them."

"Have you thought about what you will do when they get older? You can't keep them locked up on Argyle Avenue forever."

"Can't I?" Jefferson smirked. "My flower children will stay with me as long as it pleases me to keep them. After that, I can always buy new brides to replace them. Like I said, Mrs. Bigelow, on Argyle Avenue, my word is law." The commissioner stood and began to pace back and forth behind his desk. The more he talked, the louder his voice became. "Life and death are mine!" he thundered. "I am the king!"

As Jefferson continued to shout in this vein, his gestures became more erratic. A tic had sprouted underneath his right eyelid, and the pulse near his temple throbbed angrily. Though he still held the gun, it was no longer focused on Bertie. Instead, he was waving it wildly, stabbing it into the air to emphasize his point.

"I am Leroy T. Jefferson, the King of Argyle Avenue!" he bellowed. "Mine is the kingdom! Mine is the glory!"

Slowly, Bertie slid her hand into her purse. Thank God her iPhone was near the top of her bag for once. She kept her eyes fastened on Jefferson as she swiped her fingers frantically across the phone's surface. Praying she had unlocked the device, Bertie felt along the bottom and pressed what she hoped was the emergency button. The salesman at the Apple Store had assured her that this button would allow her to call 911, even if she were physically unable to punch in the correct digits. The likelihood of that happening had seemed ludicrously far-fetched at the time. But at the moment, the phone's emergency button was the only thing standing between Bertie Bigelow and certain death.

Jefferson laughed deliriously and pointed his gun at his wife's portrait. "Take that, you greedy, ballbusting whore," he shouted and fired his pistol. "No one will take my flower brides away. No one. They are mine—my jewels, my miniatures, my temples of pleasure."

As Jefferson fired another bullet in the general direction of his wife's now shattered portrait, Bertie heard a tiny voice speaking inside her purse. Hopefully, the commissioner was too deep in his mania to notice. The prissy, fussbudget bureaucrat who had met her in this office thirty minutes ago had unraveled completely. Globs of spittle formed on Jefferson's thin lips as he continued to rant in staccato phrases.

After firing another shot at Alvitra's picture, he stepped around his desk and began to walk purposefully toward Bertie.

"The time has come, Mrs. Bigelow," he said. The sudden absence of emotion in his voice was chilling. "Now that you know my story, you will understand that I have no choice but to kill you. The king has spoken."

Bertie dug frantically into her purse. Somewhere in there was the can of pepper spray Ellen had given her. *Okay, girlfriend. It's now or never.*

"Down on your knees, worthless female," Jefferson said and pointed the gun at her head.

Bertie nodded meekly, but as she slipped from her chair, she pulled the pepper spray from her purse, pointed it in the commissioner's face, and pressed the button.

Screaming in pain, Jefferson dropped the gun and lunged blindly toward her. Evading him easily, Bertie turned and ran out of the room.

Chapter Thirty-Three

Bertie was met with a round of applause when she walked into the faculty lounge three days later.

"Brava, Bertie! Hail the conquering heroine!" Maria Francione said. Taking Bertie by the shoulders, the drama teacher kissed her European-style on both cheeks.

"We were just reading about you in the *Sun-Times*," Jack Ivers said. "What a story! 'College Professor Solves Double Murder.'"

Even George Frayley offered congratulations. "We may disagree on certain matters, but no one can dispute your courage in the face of danger," the English teacher said, shaking her hand.

Unaccustomed to receiving this much attention from her colleagues, Bertie shifted from one foot to the other as she stood in the center of the room.

"It's not as big a deal as they make it out in the paper," she said. "I just reacted, that's all. Anyone in my situation would have done the same thing."

"Nonsense," Frayley replied. "The facts of the matter speak for themselves, even in this rather poorly written article. You confronted a vicious killer and brought him to justice."

"In case you are planning to write a memoir," Maria Francione added. "Just remember, I've got first dibs on the screenplay."

Bertie blushed. "Thanks, everyone. Really. I hardly know what to say."

"Don't say anything," Jack Ivers said, laughing. "Just sit back and take it in. It's not every day a person has the opportunity to alter the course of civic events. Mayor Davis has just announced he will form a committee to investigate Commissioner Jefferson's handling of several development projects. The Wabash Towers complex has been put on hold indefinitely."

"More importantly, you have rescued two Thai girls from a life of virtual slavery," Frayley added. "It says right here in the paper that Illinois Protective Services has already found new homes for the children."

George Frayley was about to comment further when he saw Ellen Simpson walk into the room. Hastily, he finished his coffee, gave Bertie a parting wave, and excused himself.

If Ellen saw her nemesis leave, she gave no sign of it. With a mischievous expression on her face, she took Bertie by the elbow and steered her into the hall. "Can we go to your office?" she said urgently. "I've found out something really big."

Despite the curious expression on Bertie's face, Ellen refused to say another word until they were alone.

"You're never going to believe this, girlfriend," she said, assuming her customary perch on the edge of Bertie's desk. "Terry Witherspoon is leaving Metro at the end of this semester."

"How is that possible?" Bertie said. "The man just got here. Doesn't he have a contract?"

"He might, but he went to see Dr. Grant and begged to get out of it. Hedda Eberhardt told me so herself—in the strictest confidence, of course."

"Of course," Bertie said drily.

"Witherspoon told the chancellor he had a family emergency. Said he was going to have to return to Minneapolis."

"You thinking what I'm thinking?"

"Damn straight," Ellen said. "The only 'emergency' that jive-ass gigolo has got going on is with his lovely wife. Bet you a million bucks she cracked the whip on his trifling behind."

"I can't say I'm sorry," Bertie said. "I hate to be mean-spirited, but the man went out of his way to stab me in the back."

"That he did," Ellen said. "But our soon-to-be-ex dean of students is not the only SOB at Metro College. For example, there's a certain gentleman on the Events Committee who definitely qualifies. I am referring, of course, to that regressive moron George Frayley. Only reason I restrained myself from giving him a piece of my mind just now was that I didn't want to spoil your celebration."

"I appreciate it," Bertie said. "He was actually quite civil to me. The guy is human, after all."

"That's debatable," Ellen said. "The underhanded jerk told the Events Committee that my Hip-Hop Poetry Conference would, and I quote, 'attract dangerous elements' to our campus." The nine copper bracelets on Ellen's right arm clanked angrily as she stood up and began to pace in tight circles around the room. "So instead of contemporary poetry in a socially relevant medium, the students are once again going to be subjected to a performance by the North Shore Poetry Society."

"Doesn't the Events Committee pick a new chairman every year?" Bertie said. "Frayley has to step down in June. Maybe you'll have better luck next year."

"I'll be shocked if anyone signs up for poetry class next year after watching the pathetic show Frayley's got planned. A bunch of blue-haired old ladies reading romantic drivel from the nineteenth century."

"I've got some news that might cheer you up," Bertie said. She waited patiently until Ellen had finished pacing. "You'll never guess who called me last night."

Ellen stuck a hand on her hip and glared. "I'm glad you're in good spirits. Goodness knows, you deserve to be. But in case you hadn't noticed, I am in no mood for games."

"Okay, okay," Bertie said, raising her arms in mock surrender. "You'd have never figured it out in a million years, anyway. Sam Willis, a.k.a. The Ace of Spades, called me up last night."

"Let me guess," Ellen said sourly. "He read about you in the paper, and now he feels bad because he yelled at you about the lawsuit."

"Something like that," Bertie said with a sheepish smile. "He's coming to Chicago tomorrow and wanted to know if I am free for lunch. He says his mama wants to meet me."

"Hold on just one second, girlfriend. Did I just hear you say you're having lunch with The Ace of Spades? The finest brother this side of Hollywood?"

"That's about the size of it," Bertie said. "And yes, I promise to call you with a full report the minute it's over."

Chapter Thirty-Four

SATURDAY, NOVEMBER 11—NOON

At precisely twelve o'clock the next afternoon, Bertie Bigelow approached the black Lincoln Town Car that waited in front of her home. A uniformed chauffeur scurried out to hold the passenger door while she climbed in. As the car glided away, Bertie spotted the O'Fallon sisters peering through their front window. She was definitely going to have some explaining to do when she got back home.

The Ace was waiting on the sidewalk in front of his mother's modest West Englewood bungalow when Bertie arrived twenty minutes later. Despite the November chill, the singer wore a pair of low-slung jeans and a sleeveless white undershirt. While his torso was perhaps not as a chiseled as it had been in his heyday ten years ago, Bertie couldn't help but notice the muscles rippling under tattoos on his arms. Three heavy gold chains hung around his neck, and his trademark wavy hair was braided in cornrows and covered by a red Chicago Bulls cap.

"Glad you could make it, Bertie. After that whole mess with the concert, I was afraid you'd be too pissed at me to come," he said, taking Bertie by the hand. "Come inside and meet my mama. She's been dying to talk to you ever since she read about you in the paper the other day."

Mrs. Willis sat in a wheelchair facing the front door. A frail, light-skinned woman in her mid-seventies, she was dressed casually in blue slacks and a matching sweater. Her gray hair had been pinned in a bun at the top of her head, bringing her high cheekbones and Native American features into sharp relief.

"A pleasure to meet you," Mrs. Willis said, extending a bony hand. "My son has been talking about you."

"He has?"

"Absolutely," she said. "It's not every day someone you know gets in the paper for solving a double murder."

"I wouldn't count on it happening again in the near future," Bertie said wryly.

Mrs. Willis laughed. "I should hope not. Samuel tells me you're a teacher?"

As The Ace hovered anxiously, Bertie took a seat on the sofa across from his mother. "I'm the choral director at Metro Community College. This will be my tenth year."

"I was a teacher myself until my heart gave out. Englewood High on West Sixty-Second Street. The kids ran me crazy, but I loved every minute of it. Tell you the truth, I'm still hoping to get back in the classroom, if I can get my doctor to agree."

"Nothing like teaching to keep you young," Bertie said. "It's hard work, but the rewards can be amazing."

Mrs. Willis turned and tapped her son on the arm. "Samuel, please tell Raquia to put the food out, would you?" As The Ace left the room, she rolled her chair closer to Bertie and stage-whispered, "My son's paying someone to babysit me. Name's Raquia. She's only twenty-one. A nice enough girl and an adequate cook, but dumb as a post, I'm afraid. Nothing on her mind but the latest episode of *Scandal*. Worse than that, she hovers. Terrified my heart's going to give out." Mrs. Willis leaned forward and looked Bertie in the eye. "What I need is less hovering and more stimulation. Please say you'll come back and visit me again."

Lunch was served in the dining room on an antique cherrywood table that must have been an heirloom. After The Ace had positioned his mother's wheelchair at the head of the table, Raquia carried in plates piled high with baked chicken, potato salad, and candied yams. As they ate, Bertie and Mrs. Willis swapped classroom anecdotes while The Ace sat at the other end of the table talking heatedly into his cell phone. From what Bertie could tell, there was some kind of problem with the sound gear he'd requested for his upcoming tour. In the middle of Bertie's story about Metro Choir's last trip to the Illinois State Choir Competition, Mrs. Willis set down her fork.

"We have a guest, Samuel," she said sharply. "Put that phone away at once."

If Bertie had talked to one of her students in that tone, she would have had a fight on her hands. But to her surprise, the man known as The Ace of Spades, a.k.a. the "finest man this side of Hollywood," nodded meekly and slid the phone into his pocket.

"Sorry, Mama," he said. "Just trying to get the details together for my tour next month."

"That may be. Nonetheless, there's no excuse for rudeness," Mrs. Willis said. "And speaking of rudeness, am I to understand that you cancelled your performance with the Metro College Choir?"

"Your son did not cancel the show, Mrs. Willis," Bertie interjected hastily. "The college cancelled it after the mother of one of my students took us to court." As The Ace looked on in amusement, Bertie gave Mrs. Willis a PG version of the events surrounding Fania Jones' lawsuit.

"You mean to say, the matter has still not been resolved?" Mrs. Willis said.

"No," Bertie replied. "There's a court hearing scheduled for some time in December. The good news is that my students will not lose out completely. I've arranged for them to sing at the South Side Museum's Kwanzaa KickStart next week."

The Ace grunted. "Always a lot of celebrities at that show," he said. "At least they'll get some TV coverage out of it. Still, I'm sorry we did not get to do the set we'd planned. And again, sorry I lost my temper, Bertie. I just hate dealing with lawyers."

Mrs. Willis wiped her mouth on a yellow cloth napkin and peered accusingly over her spectacles.

"This is all your fault, Samuel. You should never have given that girl your number in the first place. Isn't there anything you can do?"

Under his mother's stern gaze, The Ace looked down and pushed a piece of chicken across his plate.

"You're right, Mama," he said softly. "I'll look into it."

Dessert was a dish of warm peach cobbler topped with vanilla ice cream. As Raquia cleared away the last of the dishes, Mrs. Willis announced that she was tired. Taking the hint, Bertie hugged the feisty older woman and promised to visit again soon.

"You better," Mrs. Willis said. Turning her wheelchair toward the kitchen, she called out, "Come on, Raquia. Take me away from this madness. It's time for my nap."

As Bertie slid into the black Lincoln Town Car that waited for her in front of Mrs. Willis' home, The Ace kissed her on the cheek.

"I like you. You're not like the pea-brained chickenheads I usually meet," he said. "You're smart. You've got style, and you've got guts."

"Thanks," Bertie said, hoping she was not blushing too visibly.

"I'd like the chance to show you my better side. I'm going on tour, but I'll be back in January. Can I call you?"

Completely at a loss for words, Bertie smiled and nodded her head. As the limo pulled away from the curb, she pinched herself.

Not once, but twice.

Chapter Thirty-Five

Bertie listened to her classroom buzz with excitement as the students filed in and stood on the risers next to the piano. This was it. The final rehearsal before the South Side Museum Kwanzaa KickStart. As she nodded to the accompanist and the music began, Bertie sent up a silent prayer that everything would go smoothly.

Two hours later, both Bertie and her students were exhausted.

"We've been over the ending to 'Inseparable' at least ten times," Bertie said wearily, "and it is still not right." She shot a challenging glare in the direction of the ten boys in her tenor section. "How many times do I have to tell you, Maurice? There's only one bar before we go to the coda."

Maurice Green shuffled his feet and looked down at the floor. "Yes, ma'am. I won't forget next time. I promise."

"I hope not," Bertie said grimly. "The show is tomorrow."

She nodded toward the accompanist, listening intently as the choir ran through the song for what she hoped was the last time. Sure enough, Maurice and the rest of the tenors sang the ending flawlessly.

Though she was reluctant to celebrate prematurely, Bertie was pleased with her choir. The students had persevered, in spite of all the drama that had taken place during the semester. Tomorrow night, they would perform live on WGN-TV before an appreciative audience of local celebrities at the Kwanzaa KickStart.

As Bertie was about to dismiss the choir for the evening, Melissa Jones walked into the room. Dressed in a pair of impossibly tight leather pants, platform heels, and a skimpy red halter top, Melissa sauntered up to the podium and tapped Bertie on the shoulder.

"Long time no see," she said, ignoring the dirty looks being sent her way by the rest of the students. "I just stopped by to let y'all know that my mother has called off the lawsuit."

"This is wonderful news," Bertie said. "Did you hear that, everyone? The lawsuit is not going to go forward."

There was a smattering of applause. From their places on the riser next to the piano, Nyala Clark and Maurice Green continued to glare in Melissa's direction. If Melissa was going to rejoin the group next semester, Bertie knew she would need to diffuse this cloud of resentment. Hoping to lead by example, she offered Melissa her hand.

"I am glad everything is finally settled, Melissa. It will be good to have you back in the choir next semester."

"'Fraid not, Mrs. B," Melissa said. "I'm leaving next week to go on tour with Vanilla Pudding."

Nyala Clark looked like she was about to explode. Vanilla Pudding, a.k.a. Steve Steinberg, was a blue-eyed soul brother whose X-rated hit "Soft 'N' Creamy" had garnered over one million YouTube hits in the past month.

"How the hell'd you get that gig?" Nyala said. "You post your sorry little titties on Instagram?"

Melissa favored her archrival with a smug smile. "Of course not, fool. I auditioned, like everyone else. But I will say, The Ace hooked me up, though. He put in a call on my behalf. When I called to thank him for the gig, he told me to be a good girl, concentrate on my dance moves, and keep my clothes on."

Ellen Simpson laughed when Bertie told her about Melissa's visit. As was their custom, the two women were enjoying a quick drink at

Rudy's Tap before going home for the evening.

"That's just too damn much," Ellen chortled. After she'd taken another sip from her rum and Coke, her expression turned serious. "You know, The Ace got her that job as a favor to you."

"I suppose," Bertie said. "He felt bad about the way he behaved when the concert was cancelled. I guess he was trying to make amends."

Ellen raised an eyebrow. "Mama told him to do it, right?"

"As a matter of fact, Mrs. Willis did speak to him rather sharply," Bertie said. "I was surprised he didn't argue or answer back. Just said 'yes, Mama' and got right on the case."

"A Mama's Boy," Ellen said. "I know you're hot on this guy, and I will not deny that he is fine, but dating a Mama's Boy is more than a notion, Bertie."

Bertie laughed. "Don't worry, Ellen. I'll admit I was on cloud nine for a minute there. Who wouldn't be? As you just said, the man is sexy. But I've still got my feet on the ground. We'll see what happens when his tour is finished."

"Smart girl," Ellen said.

As a vintage Stevie Wonder cut pulsed from the jukebox, the two women sipped their drinks and bobbed their heads appreciatively in time to the music.

"I've got a story for you," Ellen continued. "Remember how upset I was when the Events Committee turned down my proposal for the Hip-Hop Poetry Conference?"

Bertie nodded.

"You will never guess what happened," Ellen said with a twinkle in her eye.

At that afternoon's meeting of the Events Committee, Ellen said, the North Shore Poetry Society had announced they would be changing their program. In an effort to keep pace with changing times, the group was cancelling its scheduled reading of the patriotic poems of

Henry Wadsworth Longfellow. Instead, the society intended to offer a performance of Slammin' the Bard, a spoken word mash-up of *Hamlet*, *Macbeth*, and *King Lear* set to hip-hop music.

"Frayley went ballistic," Ellen said with a grin. "For a moment there, I thought we'd have to call 911."

"Looks like you're going to have hip-hop poets after all. Here's to changing times and better rhymes," Bertie said, raising her glass in mock salute. "You going to be at the South Side Gala tomorrow night?"

"Bought a dress from Nubian Paradise just for the occasion," Ellen said with a wink. "Gonna be a lot of celebrities there. Wouldn't want those players from the Bulls to see me lookin' raggedy."

Chapter Thirty-Six

SATURDAY, NOVEMBER 18—8:00 PM

Bertie Bigelow stood near the wall, awaiting her cue. The ballroom of the Fairmont Hotel was packed. As her students lined up in rows on the makeshift stage in the front of the room, Bertie stole a glance at the glittering array of well-heeled Chicagoans who'd turned out to support the South Side Museum. Dwyane Wade from the Chicago Bulls basketball team was in attendance, as promised. So were Mayor Davis, several members of the Chicago City Council, a state senator, and a representative from the governor's office. As tuxedo-clad waiters hurried from table to table, clearing away the last dishes from an elaborate three-course dinner, the guests looked expectantly up at the stage, eager to be entertained.

It was a big moment, and a less seasoned choral director might have been terrified. But Bertie was not the least bit nervous when WGN–TV announcer Jeff Sable stepped up to the podium to kick off the evening's concert. Away from the limelight, Bertie Bigelow was a modest person, given to self-deprecation, diffidence, and attacks of acute embarrassment. Once she stepped out onto the stage, however, Bertie's inner performer took over. She was ready. Her choir was ready, and nothing was going to keep them from giving a stellar performance.

Taking a deep breath, Bertie Bigelow walked onstage and bowed deeply.

"Thank you so much, ladies and gentlemen," she said. "My students and I are proud to represent Metro Community College at this outstanding event. Tonight, we'll be performing a medley of songs made famous by three of Chicago's most famous singers: Dinah Washington, Nancy Wilson, and Nat King Cole. Sit back, relax, and enjoy the show."

Half an hour later, the entire audience was on their feet, clapping their hands and swaying to the beat as the Metro College Singers roared into the final measures of "Route 66."

Chancellor Grant greeted Bertie as she walked off the stage.

"Professor Bigelow, you are a veritable wonder worker," he enthused. "Mayor Davis wants your group to perform in Millennium Park next summer. You have put Metro College on the map!" As he pumped Bertie's hand vigorously, the chancellor continued to scan the crowd. "Is that Alderman Gordon standing by the bar? I've been trying to get in touch with him for weeks. Please excuse me."

As the chancellor bustled off to collect compliments from the politicians who oversaw the college's annual budget, Bertie spotted Charley and Mabel Howard by the bar. In honor of the occasion, the Hot Sauce King had forsaken his customary overalls and checkered shirt in favor of an Italian tuxedo. Mabel wore a flowing chiffon gown that reminded Bertie of a Hawaiian sunset.

"That was one fine shindig, little lady," Charley said. "I'm not much of a music critic, but I'd say your students hit it out of the park." After looking down at his shoes for a moment, the Hot Sauce King cleared his throat. "I owe you an apology, Bertie. What I said about you being the worst detective ever? I didn't mean it. To show you there's no hard feelings, I want you to have this."

To Bertie's absolute amazement, Charley pulled a crumpled wad of hundred dollar bills from his pocket, thrust it into her hand, and walked away.

In response to Bertie's bewildered shrug, Mabel said, "I never doubted for a minute that you would solve these murders. After all, you've got Capricorn rising and your ninth house is in Taurus. You're naturally dogged, determined, and practical." She gave Bertie a peck on the cheek. "To let you know how much I appreciate what you've done, I'm giving you a discount on your first three visits."

"Visits? What for?"

"Psychic readings, of course. Penny Swift is bringing me to Kenilworth next week for a special seminar on Psychic Self-Defense. After that, I'm booked solid until Christmas."

When Bertie gave her a skeptical look, Mabel smiled. "I know what you're thinking, Bertie. But I am as normal as you are. The doctors at Northwestern University Hospital went over me with a fine-toothed comb."

"I have to say, I was worried about you."

"I was worried about me too," Mabel said. "Spending all that money on Sister Destina when I had The Gift within me the whole time. Isn't that funny? Anyway, here's my card. Take it. You never know when it might come in handy."

Mabel's card was silver and edged with gold glitter. Printed in the center in elaborate gold letters were the words:

Mabel Howard
Psychic Medium
"The future is yours for the asking."

Bertie tucked the card and Charley's money into her purse. Uncertain what to do next, she surveyed the room. A large group from Metro College chattered excitedly at the other end of the room next to the stage. Even at this distance, Ellen Simpson, decked out in a magnificent orange and blue dress from Ghana, was easy to spot.

As Bertie crossed the room to join her friends, she noticed David Mackenzie standing alone in the corner. His tuxedo was not the most expensive in the room. And while he was a decent-looking man, Mac was too bear-like to be considered handsome. All the same, the man had a presence—the air of someone completely at home in his own skin.

In spite of her best efforts to remain calm, Bertie felt her heartbeat accelerate as she tapped the burly lawyer on the arm.

"Hello, Mac," she said softly. "I didn't know you were going to be here tonight. It's good to see you."

"Great show," he said, bending down to kiss her cheek. "Your students did an amazing job."

Angelique Mackenzie, turned out in a form-fitting sequined gown that must have set her back at least five thousand dollars, materialized next to her husband.

"I had no idea your choir was that good," she said, taking Mac protectively by the arm. Apparently, the on-again, off-again Mackenzie marriage was back on. Bertie masked her disappointment with a smile.

"We had a lot of obstacles this semester," Bertie said. "But we managed to pull it off. I'm very pleased."

"That's nice," Angelique said with a distracted nod. "Is that Graciella Bowman over there? I need to ask her about the Octagon Society Ladies' Luncheon. Excuse me, Bertie."

As Angelique hurried away, Mac and Bertie surveyed each other in silence. Finally, the lawyer cleared his throat. "Always good to see you," he said, giving her hand a plaintive squeeze. "Don't be a stranger, okay?"

As Mac walked away, Bertie surprised herself by laughing out loud. *Life is one damn storm after another,* she thought wryly. *But the sun is bound to come out eventually.*

At the far end of the room next to the stage, the Metro College contingent continued to celebrate. Nyala Clark and Maurice Green exchanged fist bumps as their parents looked on with pride. Jack Ivers thumped TyJuana Barnes enthusiastically on the back. Even George Frayley looked pleased. Maria Francione, dressed for the occasion in a low-cut scarlet gown and matching six-inch heels, blew Bertie a kiss.

"Brava, Bertie! Bravissima!" Her theatrical soprano carried easily over the noise of the crowd. "Come join us. Take another bow."

Whistling the chorus of "Be Positive" under her breath, Bertie Bigelow grinned and pushed her way through the crowd.

— *The End* —

Acknowledgements

Many wonderful people helped me to bring this book to life. My mother, Elizabeth, shared her insider's perspective on the Chicago City College system. My brothers David and Timothy patiently answered my (many) questions on legal procedure. My brother Stephen provided a boots-on-the-ground perspective of life and politics on the South Side. My beta readers—Rachel Greenberg, Eve Shalpik, Pat Murray, and Sarah Ritt—offered valuable writing advice.

A special thank-you goes to Duke and Kimberly Pennell, Meg Welch Dendler, and the rest of the Pen-L publishing team for all their hard work. And a big hug goes to my wonderful husband, John—my toughest critic, my cheering section, and my rock.

About the Author

 As a kid growing up on the South Side of Chicago, Carolyn Marie Wilkins dreamed of singing backup for Aretha Franklin while becoming the next Agatha Christie. Although she's still waiting for Aretha to call, Carolyn is now the author of five books. *Mojo For Murder* and *Melody For Murder* feature the crime-fighting exploits of Bertie Bigelow, a forty-something choir director and amateur sleuth living on the South Side of Chicago. Carolyn's nonfiction work includes *They Raised Me Up: A Black Single Mother and the Women Who Inspired Her; Damn Near White: An African American Family's Rise from Slavery to Bittersweet Success,* and *Tips For Singers: Performing, Auditioning, Rehearsing.*

An accomplished jazz vocalist and professor at Berklee College of Music, Carolyn has performed on TV and radio with her group SpiritJazz, toured South America as a Jazz Ambassador for the US State Department, and played for shows featuring Melba Moore, Nancy Wilson, and the Fifth Dimension. When she's not in the classroom or writing her next mystery novel, Carolyn can be found hanging out in the jazz clubs around Boston, Massachusetts.

Special Bonus Chapter!

DON'T MISS CAROLYN WILKINS'
MELODY FOR MURDER
~A BERTIE BIGELOW MYSTERY~

When recently-widowed college choir director Bertie Bigelow reluctantly accepts a New Year's date with Judge Theophilous Green, she never imagines the esteemed civil rights pioneer and inveterate snob will be found shot to death the next morning. She's even more surprised when her talented but troubled student LaShawn Thomas is arrested for the crime. But Bertie suspects that someone in her tight-knit social circle is really the killer.

Bertie will need to keep her wits about her to avoid becoming the killer's next victim.

PRAISE FOR MELODY FOR MURDER

In a genre replete with formula approaches and one-dimensional figures, *Melody for Murder* successfully stands out with its winding developments, vividly realistic moments, and the talents of a college professor turned sleuth who finds her good intentions repeatedly land her in the path of danger. It's highly recommended for any genre fan who wants fresh, lively writing and a protagonist who is neither beautiful nor a sleuthing genius—just a likeable, believable human being who finds herself involved in something outside her career and expectations.

– D. Donovan, Senior Reviewer, Midwest Book Review

CHAPTER ONE

"Something terrible is going to happen," Mabel Howard said. She slid into the red plastic booth across from Bertie Bigelow and frowned. "You've got to help me."

"Take a deep breath," Bertie replied. In her ten years running the music program at Metro Community College, Bertie had soothed more than her share of nervous people. "Slow down, and tell me the whole story from the beginning."

"I don't have *time* to go back to the beginning, Bertie! Charley's restaurant has been hexed. Sister Destina says the curse will take effect in six hours." Mabel Howard, a bone-thin woman with a nut-brown complexion, tore at her napkin with exquisitely manicured fingers.

Bertie sighed inwardly. Mabel was sharp as a tack, most of the time. But when it came to anything involving psychics, astrology, Tarot cards, or past lives, the woman was a total fanatic.

"Let me get this straight," Bertie said. "You went to see a psychic, and now you think your husband's restaurant has been cursed?"

"Sister Destina is not just any psychic. She's a spiritual genius," Mabel said. "Of course, she's not really a woman. Technically speaking, Sister Destina is a man, but with a lot of yin energy. He was a woman in his last two lifetimes."

Out of respect for her friend's feelings, Bertie refrained from rolling her eyes.

"Sounds like a scam to me, girlfriend," she said. Short and soft-spoken, Bertie Bigelow was just shy of forty with a full bosom, a light-beige complexion, and generous hips. "Did this Destina person give you any concrete information about the curse? Anything at all?"

Mabel glared at Bertie through tear-stained eyes. "I'm not stupid, you know. I would never have believed in the curse if my Grandma

Hattie hadn't come back from the dead to warn me. Sister Destina saw my grandmother in a vision—clear as I'm seeing you right now. No one can do that unless they have the gift."

It was just after noon, and the TastyCakes Diner was packed. Bertie flagged down a harassed waitress and ordered a tuna sandwich. Too nervous to eat, Mabel ordered coffee.

"Unless a Black Star banishing ritual is performed in the next six hours, Charley and I are as good as dead," Mabel said.

Bertie raised an eyebrow. "Have you talked to your husband about this?"

"I tried, Bertie. I tried." Mabel upended the sugar dispenser and stirred a river of empty calories into her cup. "When I told him the ritual was going to cost two thousand dollars, Charley hit the ceiling. Said he'd see Sister Destina in hell before he gave her a single dime."

Bertie suppressed a grin. Commonly known as the Hot Sauce King, Mabel's husband was a garrulous, blue-black hulk of a man, whose down-home drawl and folksy manners belied a brilliant mind. Charley Howard's Hot Links Emporium was one of the most popular BBQ restaurants on the South Side of Chicago. Bertie was certain he had not clawed his way to the top by gazing dreamily at the stars. Although he swore he'd turned over a new leaf, Charley was rumored to have gotten his start with some help from mob boss Tony Roselli.

"Two thousand dollars is a lot of money," Bertie said. "How do you know Sister Destina didn't make a mistake? Maybe she got her psychic wires crossed up or something."

"No way," Mabel said. "I've been getting chills all day. Something is out of balance in my psychic field, Bertie. I can feel it."

Bertie Bigelow chewed her sandwich thoughtfully. She didn't for one moment believe that Charley Howard's restaurant was in danger. But Mabel was her friend, and for Bertie, friends were everything. She had no children, and her husband Delroy had been killed in a hit-and-run accident eighteen months ago. Without the support of her friends, Bertie knew her own loneliness would have been unbearable.

She pushed her plate aside and leaned forward.

"Remember Francois Dumas?" she said. "The guy who owned the Club Creole on Ninety-Fifth Street?"

"Of course," Mabel said. "Charley and I used to go dancing there."

"Francois ran a great nightclub—fabulous food, live music. Only problem was, he didn't believe in paying taxes. When the IRS threatened to put him in jail, Delroy negotiated his settlement."

"I remember reading about that," Mabel said. *The Chicago Defender* called your husband the 'African-American Perry Mason.'"

Bertie smiled. "Delroy was always a little embarrassed about that. You know what a modest person he was. The point is, after the trial, Francois gave my husband a small pouch to wear around his neck."

Mabel's eyes widened. "A mojo hand?"

"I guess so. The thing is supposed to keep away evil spirits. You can borrow it if you want."

"Does it work?"

"Delroy carried it in his pocket for months, but on the day of the accident, he left it sitting on the dresser. Forgot it, I guess."

Overcome by sad memories, Bertie fell silent.

"You keep it," Mabel said. She reached across the table and squeezed her friend on the arm. "That mojo hand was made 'specially for Delroy. It wouldn't work for me, anyway."

"You sure?"

Mabel nodded. "Without Sister Destina's Black Star banishing ritual, there's nothing anyone can do."

"Tell you what," Bertie said briskly, "tonight, when I get home from work, I'll dig out the mojo hand and light a candle. Who knows? The thing could still have some whammy left."

"I could certainly use some good vibes," Mabel said with a weak smile. "I know you think I'm crazy, but mark my words, Bertie. Something bad is going to happen tonight."

FIND IT AT:

WWW.PEN-L.COM/MELODYFORMURDER.HTML

If you'd like to hear more about Carolyn's upcoming books, free deals, and other great Pen-L authors, sign up for our Pals of Pen-L Newsletter here!

WWW.PEN-L.COM/OPTIN/THANKS.HTML

Dear Readers,
If you enjoyed this
book enough to review
it for Goodreads, B&N,
or Amazon.com, I'd
appreciate it!
Thanks, Carolyn

Find more great reads at
Pen-L.com

Made in the USA
Middletown, DE
14 April 2018